WHERE LOVE Ends

WHERE LOVE ENDS, SECRETS BEGIN

LISA RENÉE RUGGERI

Copyright © 2025 by Lisa Renée Ruggeri

All rights reserved. No part of this book may be reproduced, distributed, or transmitted in any form or by any means, including photocopying, recording, or other electronic or mechanical methods, without the prior written permission of the author, except in the case of brief quotations embodied in critical reviews and certain other non-commercial uses permitted by copyright law. For permission requests, write to the author -visit the website address below for details:

www.lisareneeruggeri.com

Disclaimer:
This is a work of fiction. Names, characters, businesses, places, events, and incidents are either the products of the author's imagination or used in a fictitious manner. Any resemblance to actual persons, living or dead, or actual events is purely coincidental.

ISBN: 9798306700922
Printed by Amazon (KDP)

To my loving family...

Prologue

The sun hung low over the rolling hills of Sicily, casting a warm, golden glow across the landscape. Rows of olive trees stretched out as far as the eye could see, their leaves glinting in the fading light. The air was thick with the scent of lemons, ripening in the nearby groves, mingling with the sweetness of fig trees. It was a picture of idyllic beauty, the kind of place that tourists would one day come to marvel at. But for young Isabella, it was a prison.

At fifteen years old, Isabella already knew the backbreaking routine of farm life better than any of her brothers. She spent her days tending to the chickens, milking the goats, and helping her mother in the kitchen. Her hands were calloused from work, her dark hair always tied back in a hasty braid to keep it out of her delicate face as she moved from one chore to the next. Her brothers, on the other hand, had the luxury of going to school, their heads filled with lessons and books while she remained trapped here, bound to the farm like one of the animals she cared for.

She often found herself staring out over the fields, wishing she could be anywhere but here. She dreamed of the cities her father spoke of—Milan, Florence, Rome—places where fashion and art thrived, where women wore beautiful dresses and walked down cobbled streets lined with grand buildings, where life wasn't limited to dusty fields and endless chores.

"*Bella mia,*" her father Angelo would say whenever he caught her daydreaming, his voice warm and filled with affection. He was a kind man, with strong, weathered hands and a gentle smile. Angelo never scolded her for dreaming, unlike her mother. "One day, you'll see the world. Milan, Paris—places where fashion is born. You'll wear dresses that make people stop and stare."

Isabella's heart would flutter at his words. Her father, with his stories of big cities and grand possibilities, was the only one who understood her. He would take her aside whenever he could, speaking to her of a life beyond the farm, a life full of opportunities and beauty. But as much as Angelo encouraged her dreams, her mother was always there to snuff them out.

"Isabella!" her mother's sharp voice would call, pulling her back to reality. "Enough with your foolish fantasies. Get to work!"

Her mother was a strict woman, hardened by years of working the land. She had no patience for daydreams or idle wishes, especially from her daughter. To her, Isabella was destined for one thing: marriage. There was a man in the village—Vincenzo, the son of a local farmer—who had been chosen for her. The arrangement had been made years ago, and when Isabella turned sixteen, she would marry him, no questions asked. Her mother saw the marriage as the only way to secure their farm and future, a practical decision that had nothing to do with love.

But the thought of marrying Vincenzo filled Isabella with dread. She barely knew him, and what little she did know, she didn't like. He was surly, unkind, and had none of the spark or excitement or ambition that she longed for. She couldn't imagine spending the rest of her life with him, trapped in the same small village, on a farm just like her family's.

One evening, after a long day of work, she found her father sitting outside under the shade of the fig trees, his face softened by the evening light. She approached him, her heart heavy with fear and uncertainty.

"*Papà*," she whispered, sitting beside him. "I don't want to marry Vincenzo. I don't want to stay here."

Angelo turned to her, his expression kind but serious. "I know, *bella mia.* I know."

"Please," she begged, her voice shaking. "Don't let them make me do it. I want more than this—I want to see the world, to live, not just survive."

Angelo sighed, reaching out to gently brush a strand of hair from her face. "I will protect you," he promised, his voice steady. "You will not marry him if you don't want to. I swear it."

With thick, dark hair that cascaded down her back in waves, skin bronzed by the Sicilian sun, and eyes the color of the deep blue Mediterranean, Isabella looked like she had stepped out of one of the fashion magazines her father brought back from the city. She was tall for her age, with graceful features and a natural elegance that seemed at odds with the rough farm work she did every day. Her beauty was undeniable, and yet, she was trapped in a life that seemed too small for her.

"I don't just think you will have more than this life, Isabella," Angelo said, his voice firm. "I *know* it. Your beauty is rare, and it's not just on the outside. You have something in you that shines, something that the world needs to see. When I was a young man, I spent some time in Milan, working in the markets. I would see the women, dressed in the finest clothes, walking to fashion shows, their faces in magazines. And every time I look at you, I know that you belong there, too. You are *meant* to be seen."

Isabella looked down at her hands, the dirt under her fingernails a stark contrast to the glamorous life her father described. It felt like a faraway dream, impossible to reach from here. "But what about the farm? And *Mamma*... she would never let me leave."

"I will not let you be forced into that life," he said, his voice strong. "I want more for you. You are not meant to spend your days tending to animals and raising children on a farm, not when you have the potential to be so much more."

Isabella's heart swelled with relief, trusting her father's words. But that trust would soon be shattered.

It happened on a morning like any other. Angelo had gone out early to work the fields, as he always did. But by midday, word spread through the village—he had fallen. When Isabella rode her bike frantically back to the field, her heart pounding in her chest, she found her father's body lying still, his strong hands limp at his sides- her mother and brothers wailing as the local doctor came to check his lifeless body. He was gone.

The days that followed were a blur of grief. Isabella felt as if her world had collapsed around her. Her father, her protector, the only one who understood her dreams, was gone. And with his death, so too went his promise.

Her mother wasted no time. With Angelo gone, the farm needed saving more than ever, and the solution was clear to her—Isabella's marriage to Vincenzo would secure their future. The preparations began almost immediately, her mother and brothers arranging the details as if her own wishes didn't matter.

But Isabella couldn't bear it. Every day, she felt the walls closing in, the life she had feared becoming more and more inevitable. She couldn't do it. She *wouldn't* do it.

On a moonless night, while the village slept, Isabella made her decision. She packed a small bag with what little she had—some clothes, a few precious items her father had given her, and enough money to get as far away as possible. She stood for a moment in the doorway of her small bedroom, looking around at the life she was leaving behind. It wasn't hard to go. Not anymore. She had already lost the one person who had believed in her- she had nothing left to lose now.

She slipped out into the dark, the cool night air brushing against her skin as she made her way through the familiar fields. The scent of lemons and figs was still thick in the air, but this time it didn't feel comforting. It felt like goodbye.

Without looking back, Isabella walked into the night, her heart pounding in her chest. She didn't know where she was going, but she knew one thing for sure: she was never coming back. This life—the one her mother had planned for her—wasn't hers. She would find her own way, just like her father had always told her she could.

And so, with nothing but her dreams to guide her, Isabella disappeared into the dark, chasing a future that was entirely her own.

Angela stood at the enormous window of the penthouse, gazing out at the expanse of the city below. The streets of New York were humming, as they always did, with the sounds of cars, people, and life. But up here, thirty floors above it all, it was quiet. The kind of quiet that made the world feel far away, unreachable, like watching life through a glass you couldn't break.

The penthouse was a massive, sprawling thing, all polished marble floors and gleaming chandeliers. It was the kind of place most people only saw in magazines—the kind where everything was always in its place, so perfect it felt like a museum. Angela hated it.

She turned from the window and glanced around the living room. The leather sofas, so shiny and uncomfortable, sat untouched. No one ever seemed to use them except when her parents hosted a party, and even then, people were more interested in the champagne and the view. The fireplace, a massive marble structure that stretched halfway up the wall, had never seen a single flame. Her mother said fire made everything smell like smoke.

It was the same with the rest of the place—elegant, cold, and utterly impersonal. Nothing in the penthouse reflected Angela. Her parents had moved into this penthouse before she was even born. Her mother, Isabella, had come to America from Italy when she was just fifteen years old, with nothing but a single suitcase and a head full of dreams. That was one of the stories Isabella loved to tell when she had guests over, sitting at the head of the long dining table, her diamonds flashing in the candlelight. How she had gone from nothing to everything, married into one of the wealthiest families in New York, and was now living in a building so fancy it had its own elevator. "A real Cinderella story," her mother would say with a glossy smile, but Angela never believed it was that simple.

Her father, Daniel, had been born into wealth, the son of a real estate tycoon who had made his fortune buying up half of Manhattan. Angela had never met her grandparents—they'd died long before she was born—but their legacy was everywhere. The businesses, the properties, the estates. Her father ran it all now, barely ever home, consumed by work. He was the kind of man who thought that money could solve anything.

Angela often wondered if her father even noticed when she wasn't around. He came home late from his office downtown, sometimes not at all. When he was home, he'd hole up in his study, reviewing contracts, negotiating deals over the phone, always too busy to talk. And her mother, well, Isabella spent her time organizing charity galas, meeting with designers, or chatting with her friends about the latest gossip. Even at home, she was always dressed as if she were about to walk a red carpet. Her beauty always on show for everyone to see. Angela couldn't remember the last time she'd seen her mother in anything as ordinary as jeans.

Her sisters, all older by around five to ten years, had learned to blend into this world effortlessly. Francesca, the oldest, was already married and living in Paris with her husband, who ran an art gallery. Camilla was training to be an opera singer, while Bianca was starting law school in Boston. They were beautiful, poised, and successful, each of them their own shining example of perfection, just like their mother.

And then there was Angela.

She was fifteen now, and it felt like she didn't fit in anywhere. Not in this penthouse, not at her elite private school, and definitely not with her sisters, who seemed to glide through life as if they had everything figured out. Angela had dark, softly curled hair that framed her delicate face, accentuating her olive skin, while her striking deep blue eyes stood out in captivating contrast, giving her a unique allure—traits she inherited from her Italian mother. Unlike her tall, statuesque sisters who commanded attention with their height, Angela was petite, her figure graceful yet understated. She often felt invisible next to them, their glamorous presence making her feel even smaller in the extravagant world they lived in. While they embraced their beauty with the confidence of women who knew they were admired, Angela's quieter beauty had a gentleness about it, one that often went unnoticed in the glitzy life she was part of.

Angela's days were packed with activities, all carefully curated by her mother. Ballet classes in the morning, drama lessons in the afternoon, golf lessons on weekends, all of it designed to mold her into some perfect version of a daughter her mother seemed to want. But none of it was what Angela wanted. She didn't care about pirouettes or learning how to properly throw her voice on stage. And she definitely didn't care about golf.

What she really wanted was to be with animals. Ever since she could remember, Angela had dreamed of becoming a vet. She used to beg her parents to let her visit the zoo, not just to see the animals but to spend time with them, to learn how to care for them. But her mother had dismissed the idea. "A vet, Angela? That's not a job for someone like you. That's not what our family does."

And so, instead of spending her time with animals or learning about them, Angela was chauffeured around the city in a sleek black limo, going from one lesson to the next, always under the watchful eye of her mother's driver. Her days were so scheduled, so planned, that sometimes it felt like she was just going through the motions of someone else's life.

The only time she truly felt happy was when she escaped to Central Park. She loved wandering through the zoo, watching the animals, imagining what it would be like to take care of them. She'd often sit by the lake for hours, just watching the ducks paddle by or the squirrels dart from tree to tree. Being outside, surrounded by nature, was the only thing that made her feel free.

At school, the other girls didn't get it. They came from families like hers—rich, privileged, always dressed in the latest fashions. They didn't understand why Angela would choose to spend her free time with animals when she could be shopping on Fifth Avenue or lunching at The Plaza. But Angela didn't care about any of that. She didn't care about the designer clothes or the exclusive parties. What she wanted was something real. Something that felt honest and true, something far from the glittering but hollow world of the penthouse.

As she stood at the window, staring out at the city, Angela felt that familiar ache of loneliness. It was as if she were watching the world happen around her, but she wasn't truly part of it. She could hear the faint sounds of her mother on the phone, probably arranging another party or dinner with someone important. Somewhere in the distance, she could hear the soft clicking of her father's typewriter from his study, a sound that had become background noise in their house.

Angela pressed her forehead against the cool glass, wishing for something to change. She longed for a life that was more than this. Something with meaning, with connection. She didn't know what, exactly, but she knew it was out there, waiting for her.

Maybe this summer would be different. Maybe, just maybe, she'd find a way to escape the suffocating world of her family and discover something real. Something that was hers.

With a sigh, she stepped away from the window. The sun was setting now, casting a soft orange light over the city. It was beautiful, but it still felt distant. Out of reach. Just like everything else in her life.

Angela turned and walked down the long, empty hallway of the penthouse, her footsteps echoing on the cold marble floors.

Angela stood outside Camilla's door for a moment before knocking lightly. Her hand hovered, unsure if she should even bother. Camilla was probably on the phone again with Bradley, her latest boyfriend, and Angela hated interrupting. But then again, she didn't have anywhere else to be. She knocked twice, then pushed the door open without waiting for a response.

Camilla's room was exactly what you'd expect from someone like her—flawless. The walls were a pale pink, the kind that looked like the inside of a seashell, with perfectly framed photographs of her friends from trips to Aspen and St. Tropez. Her bed, a huge canopy draped with white, gauzy fabric, looked like something out of a magazine. Camilla herself was sprawled across it, on her stomach, her legs bent at the knees and swinging lazily back and forth. Her glossy hair cascaded over her shoulder, and her manicured fingers were tapping away on the phone.

"Yeah, Brad, totally," Camilla said into her phone, her voice sweet and airy. She didn't even glance up when Angela came in. "No, I'm serious, the Hamptons is going to be amazing this year. Pool parties every weekend. You have to come!"

Angela wandered over to the bed and sat down on the edge, bouncing slightly on the plush duvet. She gazed around the room—so neat, so put together. A stack of fashion magazines lay on Camilla's vanity, perfectly organized next to rows of expensive perfumes. Everything in its place. Everything perfect.

Camilla was laughing at something Bradley said. "Okay, yeah, I'll call you later. Ciao! Mwah!" She blew a kiss into the phone and hung up, finally turning her attention to Angela.

"What's up, Ange?" she asked, rolling onto her back, her hair fanning out behind her like she was in a shampoo commercial. She had this way of looking effortlessly beautiful without even trying, something that Angela could never figure out how to do.

Angela shrugged, picking at a thread on the duvet. "I'm bored."

Camilla raised an eyebrow. "Bored? You're always bored."

"Yeah, well, this time it's worse," Angela said, flopping back dramatically on the bed beside her sister. "I just...I don't know. I feel like we do the same thing every summer. I want to do something different this year. Something exciting."

Camilla propped herself up on her elbows, looking down at Angela with a grin. "Well, you're in luck. This summer's going to be anything but boring. We're going to the Hamptons."

Angela sighed. "We always go to the Hamptons."

Camilla shook her head, her grin widening. "No, not like this. We're going to the *new* house. The big one. Mother and Father just finished renovating it, and it's supposed to be amazing. Way bigger than the last one. Think of all the pool parties, Ange. The country club, the beach, the parties—this summer's going to be epic- the summer of 1995 is going to go down in history!"

Angela rolled onto her side, facing Camilla. "It's just going to be the same thing, though. The same people, the same parties, the same...everything." She paused, feeling a weight settle in her chest. "I just want something real. Something different."

Camilla sighed dramatically, but there was still a spark of excitement in her eyes. "Oh, come on, Ange. It won't be that bad. It'll be fun! Think about it—Bradley's coming this year, and I think he's going to ask me to the country club dance. Can you imagine? Me, the center of attention, with Bradley on my arm. It's going to be *so* perfect."

Angela forced a smile, but inside she felt even more deflated. Camilla's excitement was evident, but it was all tied to the same things Angela found empty—fancy houses, glamorous parties, and superficial relationships.

"Yeah, sounds great," Angela said, sitting up. "I guess I'll just be hanging out with the same crowd, doing the same thing as last year."

Camilla rolled her eyes playfully. "Don't be such a downer, Ange. Just try to enjoy it, okay? I mean, we're going to have this huge house, a pool, the beach...it's what every girl your age dreams about."

Angela stood up, brushing off her jeans. "Maybe," she said, noncommittal. "Anyway, I'll see you later."

Camilla's phone rang again, lighting up with Bradley's name on the caller ID. "Speak of the devil," she said, grinning as she picked up her phone. "Gotta go. Bradley needs me. You'll be fine, right?"

"Yeah," Angela said quietly, but Camilla was already lost in her conversation, giggling and tossing her hair like she was in a movie.

Angela slipped out of the room, closing the door behind her, and made her way down the hallway to her own bedroom. As she entered, the familiar sight of her cluttered desk, the scattered papers, and her unmade bed greeted her. It was the opposite of Camilla's immaculate space. But it was hers.

She grabbed her Discman from her bedside table, the sleek silver surface gleaming in the dim light, and carefully put in her favorite CD. Slipping on her headphones, she lay back on her bed and pressed play. The music filled her ears instantly, drowning out the emptiness of the penthouse, the conversations she didn't want to hear, the future she wasn't sure she wanted.

As the soft, melodic tunes drifted through her headphones, Angela closed her eyes and let herself imagine something else—something far from the Hamptons, far from the parties, far from all of it. She pictured herself in the African savanna, the golden grasses stretching out as far as she could see. The air was hot and dry, the sound of animals rustling in the distance. In her mind, she was there, helping take care of the elephants, the lions, the endangered animals that needed her. She could almost hear their calls, feel the warmth of the sun on her skin. This was where she wanted to be—out in the world, doing something real, something that mattered.

Angela smiled softly, the music and her imagination carrying her far away from the penthouse, from the Hamptons, and from everything that felt like a cage. For now, at least, she could escape.

2

The limo glided up the long, winding driveway, its tires crunching over the perfectly placed gravel as Angela gazed out the window. Ahead of them, the house loomed like a palace, framed by towering oak trees and manicured hedges. The summer sun bathed the mansion in golden light, making it look like something out of a picture-perfect postcard. Its whitewashed walls gleamed in the sunlight, and wide terraces wrapped around the house like outstretched arms, welcoming them to their luxurious summer escape. The whole place felt too perfect, too pristine—like a dream Angela couldn't quite fit into.

    Inside the limo, her sisters were already buzzing with excitement. Francesca, the eldest, sat elegantly beside her husband, Pierre, who gazed out the window with a detached expression, clearly accustomed to such grandeur. Francesca, with her blonde hair perfectly styled, hummed contentedly, already imagining the summer's social gatherings. Bianca and Camilla, seated across from Angela, were chattering away about the endless parties and events that awaited them, their tall, statuesque figures filling the space with an energy Angela found exhausting. Angela, with her petite frame and dark, softly curled hair, felt worlds apart from her glamorous sisters.

When the limo finally came to a stop, her mother, Isabella, was the first to step out, taking in the sprawling property with an air of approval. "Now this," Isabella said, smoothing down her perfectly pressed linen dress, "is a house worthy of our family." Her deep blue eyes—so much like Angela's own—scanned the house as if assessing its value, not just in terms of money, but in how it elevated their family's status.

The rest of the family followed her out of the limo. Francesca linked arms with Pierre as they headed toward the front doors, while Camilla and Bianca giggled behind them, their excitement obvious for all to see.

Angela lingered at the back, trailing behind. The house was undeniably beautiful, but she couldn't shake the feeling of isolation creeping in. It was the same feeling she'd had since she was young—an outsider in her own family. Even now, standing in front of a mansion that could rival anything on the pages of an architectural magazine, she felt like she didn't belong.

Inside, the house was more extravagant than anything Angela had ever seen. wooden floors stretched through vast hallways, and chandeliers sparkled from the ceilings, casting glittering light across the room. Enormous windows offered views of the infinity pool outside, its blue waters shimmering in the sunlight. Beyond it, the ocean stretched endlessly toward the horizon, as if inviting Angela to disappear into its depths.

"Isn't it amazing?" Camilla twirled in the middle of the grand living room, her voice echoing off the high ceilings. "Think of all the pool parties we'll have!"

Angela forced a smile. "Yeah... amazing."

But even as her sisters darted off to explore the house, Angela's heart felt heavy. The grandeur only seemed to suffocate her further, like an elaborate cage disguised as luxury.

Later, as the sun began to dip in the sky, casting long shadows across the lawn, Angela found herself on the terrace, staring out at the ocean. The waves rolled in lazily, their rhythmic crash against the shore a soothing contrast to the bustling world behind her. She wrapped her arms around herself, feeling small against the vastness of the world.

The sound of her mother's heels clicking on the tiled kitchen floor behind her shattered the momentary peace. "Angela," Isabella said, her voice sharp, cutting through the salty air.

Angela turned, already bracing herself for the inevitable confrontation. Isabella stood tall, her dark hair swept back in a sleek bun, her elegant dress perfectly pressed. Even after all these years in America, she still carried the air of her Italian roots—proud, strong, and immaculately composed.

"What's your problem?" Isabella asked, her voice cold. "You have everything a girl could want—this house, this family. You should be grateful. I didn't have any of this growing up in Italy."

Angela stared at her mother, frustration bubbling up inside her. "Yes, we have all heard about how you came from nothing! But I didn't ask for this," she said quietly.

Isabella raised an eyebrow, her expression hardening. "Oh? And what exactly is it that you want? To run off and live in the wild like some kind of... animal lover? To waste your time with foolish dreams?"

Angela looked away, her eyes drifting back to the ocean. The truth was, she didn't know exactly what she wanted. She just knew that this wasn't it—this life of parties and status and keeping up appearances. It all felt so empty.

"I just want something real," she said, her voice barely above a whisper.

Her mother let out a humorless laugh. "Real? This is real, Angela. Security, wealth—this is what matters. You'll understand that one day."

Without another word, Isabella turned on her heel and walked back inside, leaving Angela alone on the terrace once more. The air around her seemed to cool, as if even the summer breeze had turned its back on her.

Angela stood and wandered down to the beach, the cool sand slipping between her toes as she made her way toward the water's edge. The beach was vast and empty, the horizon stretching out before her in shades of orange and pink as the sun began to set. The ocean waves rolled in steadily, their sound a lullaby that drowned out the noise of the world behind her.

She sat down in the sand, pulling her knees to her chest. The sky was a masterpiece of color now, the kind that made everything feel both beautiful and insignificant at the same time.

Angela stared out at the horizon, feeling a restlessness biting at her insides. She didn't want to spend her summer like this—trapped in the same old cycle of parties, surrounded by people who only cared about how they looked and who they knew. She wanted something different. But what? The answer felt just out of reach, like the waves lapping at the shore, only to retreat before she could touch them.

Maybe, just maybe, this summer could be different. Maybe she could find something real—something that mattered.

3

That evening, Angela's father, Daniel, arrived just in time for dinner. His presence was like an orchestrated performance: the clink of his cufflinks as he adjusted his sleeves, the brisk sound of his polished shoes on the marble floor, and the murmured greetings from Maria, the head housemaid and the rest of the staff, as they lined up to wait on their every need. Angela glanced up at him from her seat at the long, elegantly set dining table. He was always impeccably dressed, his suit pressed to perfection, but there was an air of detachment about him, like he was a guest in their home rather than a part of their family.

The dining room was enormous, like everything in the Hamptons house. Massive windows framed the view of the ocean, and a chandelier hung above the table, casting a soft, golden glow over the room. The walls were adorned with expensive art pieces, their cold, abstract forms a stark contrast to the warmth Angela so desperately craved. Francesca, Bianca, and Camilla were already seated, chatting away, their voices full of excitement over the latest social gossip. Pierre sat beside Francesca, looking equally bored and unamused, only occasionally glancing up from his plate.

As the staff brought out course after course of perfectly plated food, Angela's mind wandered. Her fingers absently played with the edge of her napkin as she tried to think of a way to steer the conversation away from the usual shallow chatter.

"I was thinking," Angela began, her voice hesitant at first, "maybe we could do something different this summer. You know, explore the local towns, visit some different beaches... maybe even try surfing?" Her eyes flicked from her father to her mother, hoping for some glimmer of interest.

But there was none. Daniel didn't even look up from his plate, his attention fixated on cutting his steak with precision. It was as if he hadn't heard her at all.

Francesca snickered, casting a glance at Bianca, who smirked in return. Camilla rolled her eyes.

"Surfing?" Francesca laughed, placing her hand on Pierre's arm, her perfectly manicured nails catching the light. "Really, Angela? Can you imagine us in wetsuits?"

Camilla chimed in, "That's what the locals do, not us. Besides, who wants to get salt water in their hair?"

Angela's heart sank, but she pressed on, determined. "I just think it'd be fun to do something outside of all the usual parties. I mean, there's so much history here. We could explore the towns, maybe even—"

"Enough, Angela." Her mother's sharp voice cut through the room like ice. Isabella set her wine glass down with a soft *clink* and looked directly at Angela, her sapphire eyes narrowing. "You need to get your head out of the clouds. We're here for the season, and I've planned everything down to the last detail. Tomorrow is the brunch at the country club, and I've picked out a lovely dress for you."

Angela bit her lip, trying not to let the disappointment show on her face.

"And," Isabella continued, with an air of finality, "I had those awful sneakers of yours thrown out. Sneakers are for sports, not for the country club. You'll wear the shoes I've chosen for you."

Angela's heart dropped. "You threw them out?"

"Yes," Isabella said coldly. "They were hideous. You're a young lady, Angela. It's time you started dressing like one."

Camilla and Bianca giggled, whispering to each other, and Francesca smirked as she sipped her wine.

Angela stared at her plate, her appetite gone. Her father remained silent, completely disinterested in the conversation, too focused on his food or lost in his own world of business deals. He barely noticed her, just as he always had.

The rest of dinner was filled with gossip—who was arriving in the Hamptons that week, which families had already hosted parties, and the endless discussion of who was wearing what. Angela sat quietly, feeling more isolated with every passing moment.

After what felt like an eternity, the meal finally ended, and as the others drifted off to their respective corners of the mansion, Angela slipped away. She made her way to the kitchen, where the staff were cleaning up. She gave them all a smile as she snuck outside to the trash bins. Sure enough, her beloved sneakers were lying on top of the trash, in an amazing condition but discarded like they were nothing. Angela snatched them up, holding them close to her chest like they were the last piece of her real self.

Later that night, she lay in bed, her thoughts swirling. She couldn't understand why her parents were so cold, so disinterested in anything she cared about. Why couldn't they see her? It felt like she was living in someone else's life, surrounded by everything she should want but nothing she actually did.

For the next few days, it was the same cycle of luncheons, social events, and shallow conversations. Angela drifted through it all like a ghost, her sisters thriving in the spotlight while she felt more invisible than ever. The grand house, the polished perfection of their life, suffocated her.

Finally, one afternoon, Angela snapped. She grabbed her sneakers and her bike and pedaled furiously down the driveway, away from the mansion, away from the fancy town and its manicured lawns and immaculate beaches. Tears blurred her vision as she rode, the wind whipping through her hair. She didn't know where she was going, only that she needed to escape.

The sandy path beneath her tires eventually led her away from the perfect Hamptons world, and after what felt like hours, Angela found herself in a small, humble town. The difference was stark. The houses were smaller, worn with character. The beach here was less pristine but alive with the sounds of laughter and the energy of people simply enjoying life.

She parked her bike and wandered onto the beach, her sneakers sinking into the warm, uneven sand. Nearby, a group of kids about her age were playing with their dogs, running in and out of the surf, laughing without a care in the world. No fancy clothes, no expectations, not a stiletto in sight—just pure, unfiltered joy.

Angela watched them, mesmerized. They were so different from the polished crowd she knew. These kids were free, and it stirred something deep inside her. She felt a strange pull, like she was witnessing a world she had always longed for but never knew how to find. The sun began to set, casting what looked like a golden spotlight over the scene, and for the first time all summer, Angela felt a glimmer of hope. Maybe here, in this little town, she could find that something she was looking for.

After months of hitchhiking across Sicily, from small farms and dusty roads to the bustling streets of Messina, Isabella stood at the edge of the world, looking out across the wide port that led to the unknown. The salty air clung to her skin, and her heart pounded with both fear and excitement. She had spent nearly everything she had, bargaining her way onto a container ship vessel, not through the legitimate channels, but as a stowaway, hidden among crates and sacks, surrounded by the constant hum of engines and the endless sway of the ocean.

It was dangerous and illegal, but she had no other choice. She needed to escape. Her small village in Sicily had offered her nothing but heartache, and she had vowed never to return.

Now, after weeks at sea, feeling more exhausted and lost than ever, she finally stepped off the boat and into Manhattan.

The place hit her like a storm. It was 1965, and the city was alive with movement—taxis honked incessantly, the streets were packed with people, and towering buildings rose high above her, seeming to touch the sky. The air was a strange mixture of gasoline, street food, and smoke. Everything about it was chaotic, unfamiliar, and yet... thrilling. It was nothing like the quiet, sun-soaked countryside she had left behind.

Isabella's steps were unsteady as she walked through the streets. She felt like a speck of dust among a sea of people. Cars zipped by, horns blaring, and the tall buildings cast long shadows over the sidewalks. The rhythm of the city was unlike anything she had ever known. She had heard of New York before—her father's letters that he kept from her Aunt had described it as a place of opportunity and dreams. But they never mentioned how loud it was, how cold the people seemed, how everyone moved with purpose, while she wandered aimlessly, feeling small and invisible.

She was only days away from her sixteenth birthday, and she had never felt more alone.

Her hand instinctively went to the only thing that felt familiar in this new world—her father's old letters. They were yellowed with age, crinkled at the edges, but they were her lifeline. Her father, Angelo, had been her guide, her protector, and all she had left was in those letters- written by her Zia Rosa, who had left Sicily long before Isabella was born. Zia Rosa had begged Angelo to join her when she left just before World War 2, but at the time, Isabella's mother, Caterina, had just found out she was pregnant with their first child, Franco. So they stayed. But the letters continued—Zia Rosa describing her new life in America, building a home, and eventually starting her own business. Her father would always speak of her with pride, calling her "La forza della famiglia," the strong one of the family.

But the letters had stopped coming years ago. Isabella wasn't sure if Zia Rosa was still alive, or if she was even in the city anymore. All she knew was that Rosa had started a deli—*Rosa's Deli*. That was her only clue.

Isabella wandered the streets of Manhattan for hours, searching through directories, asking strangers in broken English if they knew of *Rosa's Deli*. She had almost given up hope when finally, someone pointed her in the direction of the deli's flagship store, explaining that it had become a small chain of Italian delis scattered throughout the city. Isabella couldn't believe her ears. Her Zia Rosa had built something grander than she had ever imagined.

When she arrived at the deli, her heart stopped. The smell hit her first—warm bread, garlic, the faint scent of olives, and the unmistakable aroma of prosciutto. It smelled like home. It smelled like her father. Tears pricked at the corners of her eyes, and she paused at the door, afraid to step inside, afraid of what she might find.

Pushing open the door, she stepped into a bustling sandwich shop. People were lined up, chatting in quick bursts of English and Italian, ordering thick sandwiches stuffed with meats, cheeses, and fresh vegetables. The counters gleamed, and the walls were adorned with black-and-white photographs of Italy, landscapes she recognized from her childhood.

In the corner, behind the counter, stood a small, round woman with her hair pulled into a neat grey bun. Her hands were busy slicing thin pieces of prosciutto with precision, but there was a tiredness in her movements, a slow, deliberate grace. Her skin was weathered and worn, but it was her eyes—those deep, knowing eyes—that made Isabella's breath catch in her throat.

It was like seeing a ghost. The resemblance was uncanny—Zia Rosa looked just like her father, Angelo. The same sharp eyes, the same determined set of the jaw. For a moment, neither of them spoke. They just stared at one another across the bustling deli, frozen in time.

Then, as if the years had melted away, Zia Rosa smiled softly. "Isabella," she said, her voice rough but warm, "I've been expecting you."

Isabella's heart swelled. She took a shaky step forward, feeling like she was finally home, even in this foreign land. She couldn't believe it—Zia Rosa had recognized her instantly, as though she had been waiting for this moment.

Zia Rosa wiped her hands on her apron and came around the counter, her arms outstretched. "Come here, cara," she said, pulling Isabella into a tight embrace. The smell of prosciutto and bread mingled with the familiar scent of soap and lavender, and Isabella felt the weight of her journey fall from her shoulders as she buried her face in her aunt's shoulder.

"I got a letter," Zia Rosa whispered, her voice low and full of emotion. "From your mother, Caterina. She wrote to me months ago, telling me you had run away. That you were to be married to save the farm. I knew you'd come here. It was only a matter of time."

Isabella looked up, her voice trembling. "I had no other choice, Zia. I couldn't stay. I couldn't marry that man." Her voice broke as she remembered the night she left, the desperate whispers in the dark, the fear gnawing at her chest.

Zia Rosa cupped Isabella's face in her hands, her expression fierce but tender. "You did the right thing, Isabella. You're too young, too beautiful for a life like that. Your father knew it too. He wanted so much more for you. I see it in your eyes—you look just like Caterina did when we were young, but you have Angelo's fire."

Zia Rosa's words washed over her like a balm, soothing the ache in her heart. For the first time in months, Isabella felt hope. She wasn't alone. She had made it to New York, and she had found her family. The rest, she knew, would come in time.

5

Angela wasn't sure how long she sat there, just watching, when one of the boys caught her eye. He had a relaxed, easygoing look about him, with sun-bleached hair falling in messy waves over his forehead and dark, mysterious eyes that seemed to be full of life. He jogged toward her, kicking up sand with every step, his smile wide and genuine.

"Hey," he said as he stopped in front of her, slightly out of breath but still grinning. "Are you going to just sit there watching us this whole time or are you gonna join in?"

Angela felt her heart flutter. She glanced down, momentarily unsure of what to say. "Oh, I... I don't want to intrude."

The boy shrugged, laughing lightly. "You're not intruding. We're just goofing around. Besides, you look like you could use some fun." His grin was infectious. "I'm Jared, by the way, but my friends call me Jay."

"I'm Ella," she said quickly, feeling a sudden surge of excitement mixed with nerves as she offered the name that felt more like a protective shield than a lie. She wasn't ready to be Angela here. Not yet.

"Nice to meet you, Ella," Jay said with a nod, his tone easygoing. He gestured behind him toward the group still tossing the frisbee and running through the waves. "You wanna join us? It's just a bunch of us locals hanging out. You staying nearby?"

"Yeah, sort of," Angela replied, careful not to reveal too much. "I'm just here with my family for the summer. We're staying at a hotel."

Jay raised an eyebrow but didn't question her further. Instead, he held out a hand to help her up. "Come on, Ella. Let's see if you're any good at frisbee."

Angela hesitated for a split second, then reached up to take his hand. The warmth of his grip steadied her nerves, and before she knew it, she was on her feet, jogging alongside him toward the others.

"Hey, everyone, this is Ella," Jay called out to the group as they turned to look at her. "She's joining us for a bit."

They waved and smiled, welcoming her with easy nods and hellos. No one seemed to care where she came from or who she was. There were no formal introductions and for the first time in what felt like forever, Angela didn't feel like she had to prove herself.

The game continued, and Angela quickly realized she wasn't exactly the best at frisbee. Every time she threw the disc, it either sailed wildly off course or dropped short of its mark. The others laughed—not at her, but with her—making jokes about their own clumsy throws. Jay noticed her struggle and jogged over with a chuckle.

"Here, let me show you," he said, taking the frisbee from her hands. He positioned himself behind her, his arms reaching around to show her the proper grip. "You have to flick your wrist like this," he said, guiding her hand in a fluid motion. His touch was light, but enough to make her skin tingle.

Angela tried again, and while her throw wasn't perfect, it was much better than before. The group cheered as it sailed through the air, and Angela couldn't help but laugh, a genuine sound that felt foreign to her. It wasn't forced or polite, but real—just like the carefree kids she was now standing among.

Just then, a large sandy-colored dog came bounding over, barking playfully as it ran circles around Jay and Angela. Angela crouched down, her heart immediately swelling with affection for the animal. "Who's this?"

"That's Casper," Jay said, kneeling down beside her. "He's usually pretty shy around new people, but looks like he likes you."

Casper sniffed Angela's hand, his big brown eyes locking onto hers before leaning into her with a gentle nudge. Angela felt a warmth spread through her chest as she stroked the dog's soft fur.

"I love dogs," she murmured, scratching Casper behind the ears. "I've always wanted one."

Jay smiled, watching the interaction with amusement. "Yeah? Well, you're doing something right. He doesn't usually warm up this fast."

The sun started to dip lower on the horizon. The kids played for a while longer, tossing the frisbee back and forth, Casper bounding after it with joy. Angela couldn't remember the last time she felt so free, so unburdened by expectations and appearances.

Eventually, the group settled down on the sand, watching the waves roll in as the sky turned shades of orange and pink. Jay plopped down beside her, his long legs stretched out in front of him, Casper lying contentedly at his feet.

"So, Ella," Jay said, turning to face her with an inquisitive look in his dark eyes, "where are you from? You don't seem like you're from around here."

Angela hesitated. She had to be careful, not wanting to reveal too much. "I'm just here for the summer. My family moves around a lot."

Jay nodded, accepting her vague answer. He didn't press, but there was something in the way he looked at her that told her he wasn't entirely convinced.

"I get it," he said after a moment. "A lot of people come here in the summer. The town gets taken over by tourists and rich folks. It's busy now, but when they leave, it's a whole different place. Quieter. More... real."

Angela smiled faintly, but there was a heaviness in her chest. She wanted to ask him more about his life here, about what it was like when the crowds disappeared, but she wasn't sure how. So instead, she just sat there, watching the waves crash against the shore.

"It's getting late," she said after a while, standing up and brushing the sand off her legs. "I should get going."

Jay stood too, his hands tucked into the pockets of his worn jeans. "You coming back tomorrow?" he asked casually, but there was a hint of hopefulness in his tone.

"Maybe," Angela replied with a small smile. "What's happening tomorrow?"

"We've got a festival at the beach," Jay said, grinning again. "It's kind of a big deal around here. You should come. It'd be fun."

Angela nodded, feeling a strange pull to this place, to these people, to him. "I'll try," she said softly, before picking up her bike and riding away, the wind tugging at her hair as she pedaled down the sandy path, her heart lighter than it had been in years.

The days that followed were unlike anything Angela had ever experienced. The mornings began with a nervous excitement, the kind that fluttered in her chest as soon as she opened her eyes. Every day, she'd bike down the winding sandy path that led out of her family's pristine world and into Jay's—the town, the beach, the locals. Each pedal stroke took her farther from the stifling elegance of the Hamptons and deeper into a place where she felt free.

Jay and his friends welcomed her without question. She found herself blending into their lives with ease, joining them for their small adventures around town. They showed her hidden spots—secret coves along the beach where they could swim without tourists, a cliffside overlook with the most breathtaking view of the sunset, and the old lighthouse where they'd sneak up to the top for an unspoiled view of the ocean. Every day was something new, something exciting. They built bonfires in the evenings, roasting marshmallows and telling stories beneath the stars. The simple pleasure of feeling the warmth of the fire and listening to the crackle of wood was a world away from the stiff cocktail parties she was used to. It was better. It was raw.

With each passing day, Angela felt a sense of freedom she'd never experienced before. For the first time in her life, she didn't have to worry about appearances or what people thought of her. There were no polite smiles or forced conversations about designers or country club events. Here, she could just be Ella—a girl who wanted to run barefoot in the sand, laugh until her stomach hurt, and feel the cool ocean breeze on her face. No one knew about her family's wealth, the penthouse, or the endless social obligations. She wasn't Angela Hastings, daughter of New York's elite. She was Ella, and it felt perfect.

Jay was at the center of it all. They were inseparable, their connection deepening with each passing day. Whether they were biking through town, splashing in the surf, or sitting by the fire, there was an easy flirtation between them. It was in the way Jay's hand would brush against hers as they walked, in the teasing remarks that always made her smile, in the way he looked at her, as if she were the only person on the beach. It sent shivers down her spine, a new sensation she couldn't fully describe, but one she felt herself falling into more each day.

One afternoon, as they lounged on the beach after a swim, the conversation turned to their lives. It started casually enough, with jokes and light banter, but then Jay asked a question that caught her off guard.

"So, what's your deal, Ella?" he said, leaning back on his elbows, the sun highlighting the streaks of blonde in his messy hair. His dark eyes studied her carefully. "You never really talk about your family."

Angela hesitated, her heart quickening. She'd been so careful not to reveal too much. She didn't want them to know she came from the world of the Hamptons, where people like Jay and his friends were only seen when they were serving cocktails or mowing the lawns of the estates. But something about Jay made her want to open up. Maybe it was his laid-back attitude or the way he looked at her without judgment. Or maybe it was the fact that she was growing tired of hiding.

"My family's... complicated," she said slowly, picking at the sand with her fingers. "My Father, he... he's just not around much. He's busy with work. And when he is home, it's like I don't even exist to him."

Jay's gaze softened. "That sucks. Sounds like a tough situation."

Angela nodded, her throat tightening. "Yeah, it is. My mother... she's not much better. She's more concerned with how everything looks—especially me. I think sometimes she cares more about how I appear than who I actually am."

Jay was silent for a moment, processing her words. Then he looked out toward the ocean, his jaw tightening. "Sounds rough. But at least you've got all that money, right?" His voice wasn't sarcastic, but there was an edge to it.

Angela didn't respond, not right away. She wanted to tell him that the money didn't matter, that it never made her happy. But she didn't. Instead, she just shook her head slightly.

Jay's expression softened again, and he gave a small sigh before speaking. "I guess we've all got stuff we deal with. My mom... she's everything to me. But man, she's had it rough. Raised me on her own. My dad ran off before I was even born. She's been working for some big real estate company, secretary stuff, you know. It's hard, though. Around here, people like us, we don't get much of a break. Most folks work for the rich people, and a lot of them... well, they're not exactly fans."

Angela felt a pang of guilt. She knew what "rich people" meant to someone like Jay. She bit her lip, hoping he wouldn't ask more questions about her background.

"She doesn't let me hang out around the Hamptons crowd," Jay continued, giving her a sidelong glance. "Says it's not our world, and she doesn't want me getting involved with it. I get it, though. She's been through a lot. Always working, always doing her best to make sure I'm taken care of. She's only recently met an amazing guy, too. He seems like a great man-genuinely cares about her and is even a bit interested in me. It's early days but I just want my mum to find the happiness she deserves."

There was a sadness in his voice that tugged at Angela's heart. She couldn't imagine what it must have been like for him, growing up without a father, watching his mother struggle day after day. And yet, he had this easygoing nature, this lightness that made everything seem okay.

"I'm lucky, though," Jay added, his voice softer. "My mom's always been there for me. She's tough, but she's kind. I wouldn't trade her for anything."

Angela felt her chest tighten with emotion. She admired Jay's honesty, his loyalty to his mother, and the way he seemed to handle everything with such grace. She was falling for him—harder than she ever thought possible. The way he listened to her, the way he spoke about his life, it was all so different from what she knew. There was no pretense with him, no games. Just real, raw connection.

As the sun started to set, and the birds began to fly home for the night, Angela realized she didn't want this week to end. She didn't want to go back to the world of country clubs and fancy dresses. All she could think about was Jay—the way he laughed, the way he looked at her, and how everything felt effortless with him.

That night, after another day of adventure, Angela lay in bed staring at the ceiling. Her mind was full of thoughts of Jay, his gentle smile, his deep, thoughtful eyes, and how he made her feel more alive than she ever had before. She thought about the fun they'd had with his friends, the laughter, the freedom of being herself—no masks, no expectations.

She couldn't get him off her mind, with his kind heart and simple dreams. He wasn't like the boys from her world. He was better.

Angela smiled to herself, knowing that tomorrow couldn't come fast enough. She wasn't sure where this summer was going to lead her, but one thing was certain: she wasn't ready to say goodbye to the freedom she'd found. Or to Jay.

7

Angela had become an expert at sneaking out. It wasn't hard, really. Her mother and sisters were so absorbed in their social calendars, shopping trips, and endless discussions about who wore what to the latest luncheon that her comings and goings were barely noticed. As long as she was home in time for whatever event her mother deemed important, they didn't ask too many questions.

That morning, as she stood by the front door, ready to slip out and meet Jay and the others at the beach, Isabella appeared in the hallway. Dressed in a perfectly tailored linen suit, her hair swept back elegantly, her mother looked her over with a disapproving eye.

"Angela," Isabella called, her voice sharp. "I hope you remember we're hosting the Gala tonight. It's a very important event for your father's business associates. You'll need to be dressed and ready by six. No excuses."

Angela's heart sank, the weight of her family's expectations crashing back into her like a tidal wave. She nodded, trying to keep her expression neutral. "I'll be back in time," she said, though the words felt hollow.

Her mother's eyes looked at her intensely, as if she didn't quite believe her. "See that you are. I don't need you running off like your father, always late or absent when it matters most." Isabella's tone was icy, and Angela felt the sting of her words. She had heard this complaint about her father countless times. How he was unreliable, always choosing work over his family, never showing up to the important events.

Angela bit her tongue, nodded again, and slipped out the door, her heart pounding. As she hopped on her bike and started the ride toward the beach, a familiar rush of freedom filled her veins. The wind whipped through her hair, and the weight of her mother's disappointment began to lift, if only for a few hours. She couldn't deal with that life right now. She needed to be with Jay and his friends, the only people who made her feel like she could breathe.

When she arrived at the beach, the group was already there, gathering driftwood for the bonfire. The sky was a brilliant blue, and the salty ocean air felt like a balm to her soul. Jay spotted her first, flashing that easy, charming smile that always made her heart skip a beat.

"There she is! Right on time," he called, waving her over. His dog, Casper, wagged his tail excitedly, bounding over to greet her as if she were an old friend.

Angela smiled, crouching down to pet the sandy-colored Labrador. "Hey, buddy," she said softly, her fingers ruffling the dog's fur. Casper nudged her hand, clearly happy to see her. It still amazed Jay how quickly his dog had taken to her.

As the group finished preparing for the bonfire, Angela watched all the friends interact as the navigated the task of creating the giant structure. Liam was throwing the logs at the top. He was a tall, lanky boy with shaggy brown hair and a mischievous grin that rarely left his face. He had a sarcastic sense of humor and loved to challenge Jay to competitions—whether it was surfing, biking, or who could light the bonfire the fastest. Despite his constant teasing, Liam was fiercely loyal and had a knack for lifting the group's spirits with his antics.

Next to him was Derek, a more quiet and thoughtful type. He was built strong, with short black hair and a sharp jawline, and had an air of calm that balanced out Liam's wild energy. Derek was the one who usually came up with the plans for their little adventures, always thinking things through before they acted. He didn't say much, but when he did, people listened.

The two girls in the group were Maddie and Sophie. Maddie was a whirlwind of energy, her strawberry-blonde hair always in a messy ponytail. She had a contagious laugh and an outspoken nature that made everyone feel at ease. Maddie was the one who'd start the singing, dancing, and laughter at the bonfires, and everyone else would follow.

Sophie, on the other hand, was quieter, almost shy, but she had a sharp wit once you got her talking. Her dark, curly hair framed her pale face, and she always had a book tucked under her arm. Sophie preferred to sit back and watch, occasionally tossing out a clever remark that would have the whole group laughing. But she was warm and kind, and Ella instantly felt at home around her.

Together, they felt like a family—a real one. The kind that did fun, spontaneous things together. They didn't care about appearances or who had what, and that made Ella feel lighter than she'd ever felt before.

The bonfire crackled to life as the sun began to set. Derek brought out his guitar, strumming a familiar tune, and soon everyone was singing along, their voices carried by the ocean breeze. Ella couldn't sing well, but that didn't stop her from joining in, laughing as she stumbled over the words.

Jay sat next to her, his knee brushing against hers in that casual, effortless way he always did. Every touch, every glance, made her stomach flutter. There was something about him that made her feel alive, like the rest of the world didn't matter when he was around.

"You're getting better at frisbee," Jay said with a smirk, nudging her with his shoulder. "I almost didn't have to save you this time."

Ella laughed, rolling her eyes. "I'm a fast learner."

The night passed in a blur of music, laughter, and dancing around the fire. For a few brief hours, Angela forgot about the Gala, forgot about her mother's sharp words and the world waiting for her back at the Hamptons. Here, she was free. Free to laugh, to sing, to be Ella.

But as the bonfire started to die down, the weight of her other life began to creep back in. She glanced at her watch—she was running out of time.

"I... I have to go," she said suddenly, standing up and brushing the sand off her jeans.

Jay looked at her, confused. "Already?"

"Yeah, sorry," she muttered, grabbing her bike and throwing a quick wave to the rest of the group. "I'll see you tomorrow, okay?"

Jay's eyes lingered on her for a time, concern flickering in them. "You sure everything's alright?"

"Yeah, totally fine," she lied, her heart racing as she pedaled away from the beach, guilt eating at her. She hated leaving like this—abruptly, without an explanation. But she couldn't tell them the truth-how she was from the richest family in New York. Not yet.

As she rode home, the cool night air brushing against her face, her mind wandered back to Jay. The way he smiled at her, the way he made her laugh. She felt something for him, something strong, and it scared her. How could she keep up this double life—being Angela Hastings by day and Ella by night? How long could she hide the truth?

By the time she got home, it was well past the start of the Gala. The house was still filled with people, laughter and conversation spilling out into the night air. Maria opened the back door and Angela snuck in through, hoping to slip upstairs unnoticed. But her disheveled appearance—sand still clinging to her hair and clothes—made it hard to blend in.

She barely made it two steps before she felt her mother's eyes on her. Isabella's face was a mix of shock and fury. Her mother grabbed her by the arm, pulling her to the side. "What on earth are you wearing?" she hissed, her voice low but deadly. "You look like you've been rolling in dirt. We have guests, important guests, and this is how you present yourself?"

Angela opened her mouth to explain, but Isabella didn't let her.

"You are becoming just like your father," Isabella snapped, her voice cold and cutting. "Unreliable, selfish. This is not how I raised you, Angela. I will not have you embarrassing me like this again."

Angela felt the sting of her mother's words. She knew it was coming, but it didn't make it hurt any less.

"You're grounded," Isabella declared, her voice like ice. "For the next few days. No more disappearing. No more running off. You will stay here and act like the daughter of this family."

Angela nodded, the words she wanted to say—words of anger, words of defiance—stuck in her throat. She felt small, like she always did in front of her mother. Defeated, she walked away, heading up to her room without another word. But as she lay in bed that night, staring at the ceiling, all she could think about was Jay, the beach, and the life she was so desperately trying to keep secret.

8

Angela lay on her bed, the pillow damp with tears, staring at the ceiling as the sounds of the party below faded into the night. She could hear the faint murmur of the last guest saying goodbye, followed by the soft click of the front door closing. Her heart was heavy, her chest tight, and the hurt felt like it was suffocating her.

Footsteps echoed in the hallway outside her room, deliberate and slow, unmistakably her mother's. Angela held her breath, her body tense, knowing what was coming. There was a knock at the door—a soft, but sharp sound that pierced through the quiet.

"Angela," her mother's voice called from the other side. Without waiting for a reply, the door creaked open, revealing Isabella in her elegant evening gown, her face still set in a mask of composed disapproval.

Isabella stepped inside, her eyes scanning the room before landing on her daughter. Angela sat up, wiping her face with the back of her hand, trying to conceal the tears she had no energy left to hide.

"I don't know what's gotten into you," Isabella started, her voice calm but cold. "Your behavior tonight was completely unacceptable. I was embarrassed in front of our guests, Angela. You need to start acting like the young woman you are, not some...some rebellious child."

Angela felt the words hit her like stones. She swallowed hard, trying to keep her voice steady. "I didn't mean to embarrass you, Mother. I just—"

Isabella cut her off. "You'll be staying home for the next few days. No more running off to wherever it is you go. You need to start acting responsibly, and that begins with staying put."

Angela's heart sank. "No, Mother, please..." she begged, her voice shaking. "Please don't do this. I need to get out. I—"

"You need to learn some discipline," Isabella interrupted again, her arms crossed. "This isn't up for debate."

Angela could feel the anger rising in her, her face flushing hot with frustration. "What do you think I've been doing, Mother?" she snapped, her voice louder now, cutting through the tension in the room. "Do you even care where I go or what I do? You don't care about me at all, do you?"

Isabella's gaze hardened, her expression growing colder. "I care about what kind of influences you're surrounding yourself with. Are you hanging out with people who aren't...appropriate?" She raised an eyebrow, as if the idea of Angela being around anyone outside their circle was unthinkable.

Angela's voice trembled as she looked her mother straight in the eye. "I'm just trying to find somewhere I belong. Somewhere I can be myself without...without having to be perfect for you all the time."

Isabella's eyes narrowed, as if she didn't recognize the girl standing before her. "You have everything anyone could ever want," she replied, her voice sharp. "A beautiful home, a family that provides for you, clothes, trips, whatever you need. What more do you want, Angela? What could possibly be missing?"

Angela couldn't hold it in any longer. The pain, the frustration, all of it burst out of her like a dam breaking. "Love!" she screamed, her voice raw and filled with years of hurt. "Why don't you love me? You don't even love me!"

Isabella blinked, stunned by her daughter's outburst. "Don't be ridiculous," she said, her voice wavering just slightly, though she quickly tried to regain her composure. "Of course I love you. We both do—your father and I."

"No, you don't!" Angela cried, her voice breaking. "You and Father don't care about me at all. You care about your parties, about what people think of us, about keeping up appearances. But you don't care about me! You don't even see me!"

Isabella's face grew pale, and for a moment, she stood frozen, staring at her daughter as if she didn't recognize her. Angela's words echoed through the room, hanging in the air like a weight neither of them could lift.

"You have everything anyone could ever want," Isabella repeated, though this time her voice was softer, almost pleading. "Stop being so ridiculous, Angela."

Angela shook her head, tears streaming down her face now, her voice quieter but still fierce. "That might be true," she whispered, "but I have everything...except my parents' love and attention. And that's all I've ever wanted."

The room fell silent. Isabella stood there, her face unreadable, the tension between them thick and suffocating. For the first time, Angela saw something flicker in her mother's eyes—something that looked like hesitation, maybe even regret.

Isabella opened her mouth to speak but said nothing. Instead, she turned and walked to the door, her hand resting on the handle for a long, agonizing moment. Then, without another word, she left, the soft click of the door closing behind her.

Angela sat in the quiet, her body trembling from the confrontation, her heart aching. She stared at the door, waiting for it to open again, for her mother to come back and say something—anything—that would make her feel less alone.

But the hallway remained silent.

And once again, Angela found herself in the same place she always did: alone in a house full of people who didn't see her at all.

For the next few days, Angela's world shrank to the small patch of sand where she sat each afternoon, staring out at the endless blue of the ocean. Worry gnawed at her. *What if Jay and the others think I don't like them anymore?* She hadn't had any way of contacting them. There were no phones, no way to explain why she'd suddenly disappeared. The silence from her mother only made it worse—Isabella was punishing her in more ways than one, and Angela could feel the weight of her absence in every cold glance or ignored request.

On the third day of her confinement, she sat on the beach, her knees tucked up to her chest, her mind swirling with thoughts of Jay, Liam, and the rest of the group. She missed the freedom, the laughter, the warmth of the bonfires. They had shown her a side of life that she had never known existed, and now, it felt like it was slipping away.

Suddenly, something caught her eye in the distance. A large group of people was heading toward her, their figures growing more distinct as they got closer. Angela squinted against the sun, her heart skipping a beat when she recognized the unmistakable floppy hair of Liam and the broad, strong figure of Jay leading the way.

She stood up, a burst of adrenaline rushing through her as they approached. Her heart pounded in her chest. *They found me.*

Without thinking, she ran toward them, her feet sinking into the hot sand. As soon as she reached them, they enveloped her in a tight group hug, laughter and relief filling the air. Jay, Liam, and the rest of the friends looked genuinely happy to see her, their faces full of warmth that made Angela's heart swell.

"Where have you been?" Liam asked, his voice filled with concern. "We've been looking for you everywhere. We thought something had happened."

"We've been searching the beaches every day," Jay added, his dark eyes locking onto hers, a mixture of relief and something deeper reflected in them.

Angela felt truly touched by their worry. These kids—her friends—had only known her for a few weeks, yet they cared for her in a way that felt real, genuine. It was something she had been missing in her life, and she realized just how much she had come to love their company.

"I'm so sorry," she said, her voice soft but filled with gratitude. "I got grounded. Missed some dumb family party and my mother wouldn't let me leave the house."

"That sucks," one of the girls, Maddie, said, shaking her head. "We thought maybe you didn't want to hang with us anymore."

"Are you kidding? I've been going crazy not seeing you guys," Angela replied. "But I'll be back tomorrow. My punishment's over, and I'll be free again."

The group cheered, and Liam let out a mock howl of excitement, causing everyone to laugh. One of the other boys, Derek, glanced around at the posh beach with wide eyes, taking in the grand beach houses and the impeccably kept sand.

"Wow," he said. "This place is... fancy."

Maddie nodded in agreement, brushing a strand of her windswept hair from her face. "I've never been to this part of town. It's like a different world."

Angela smiled, but there was a sadness in her eyes. "It might look lovely and fancy, but... it's all so cold and heartless around here. Trust me, it's not what it seems."

Jay, who had been quiet for a second, gave her a look—one filled with affection and a quiet understanding. It was as if he could see the weight she carried, the pressure of living in a world that wasn't really hers. His dark, mysterious eyes locked onto hers, and Angela felt a sense of relief wash over her. *He gets it,* she thought. *He gets me.*

They spent the next few minutes chatting, laughing, and planning for the next day. Jay told her about a beach BBQ they were going to have, and everyone agreed that it wouldn't be the same without her. Angela promised she'd be there, and as they said their goodbyes, her heart felt lighter, warmer.

As she watched them walk away, Angela couldn't help but feel a sense of belonging that had always eluded her before. Even though her world was full of wealth and privilege, she had never felt more at home than she did with her new friends.

From the window of their beach house, Isabella stood with her arms crossed, her face unreadable. She watched the group below, her eyes narrowing slightly as she took in the sight of her daughter laughing and hugging those kids—kids she didn't recognize, and certainly not the kind of people she wanted Angela associating with.

A flicker of concern passed over Isabella's face, followed by a tinge of disappointment. *What is happening to my daughter?* she wondered, shaking her head as she turned away, leaving Angela to her own world—one that Isabella no longer understood.

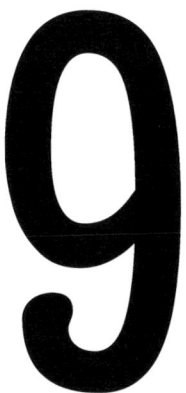

Zia Rosa was overjoyed to see her niece standing before her. It was as though the past had returned to her in the form of young Isabella—so thin, pale, and weary from her long journey. Without hesitation, she shut the deli early, hung the "Closed" sign on the door, and ushered Isabella inside.

"Sit down, bella," Zia Rosa said in her warm, Sicilian-accented voice. She quickly busied herself, slicing fresh bread, adding prosciutto, cheese, and roasted peppers, crafting a sandwich as large as Isabella's hand. When she placed it in front of her, Isabella's stomach growled in response.

"Eat, eat! You look like you haven't had a proper meal in weeks!" Rosa exclaimed, her hands flying to her hips as she watched Isabella devour the sandwich, her face softening with affection.

The hours slipped away as they sat together, catching up on all that had passed. Isabella felt safe for the first time since her father's death, spilling out her worries, her hopes, and the secret she had carried in her heart since leaving Sicily.

"Zia Rosa," Isabella began hesitantly, "please... you can't tell Mamma I'm here. She won't understand. She'll just make me come home... to marry Vincenzo. I can't do it, Zia. I don't love him. I never will."

Rosa's brow furrowed, the lines of age deepening in her face. "I understand, cara," she said, her voice gentle. "Your mother... she always had such firm ideas about life. But you... you are your father's daughter. You have dreams bigger than that little village."

Isabella's eyes shimmered with tears as she nodded. "Papa knew... he always said I wasn't meant to stay there. He believed in me. He thought I could be like the girls in Milan, walking in beautiful dresses, living a life of my own. Not just some wife. My mamma would tell me how my beauty was a curse, not a blessing."

"Your papa was a wise man," Zia Rosa said softly, reaching across the table to squeeze Isabella's hand. "And I believe in you too. You don't need to worry. I'll take care of you. You'll stay here with me. You'll work in the deli—room and food in exchange for your help."

Isabella smiled through her tears, a weight lifting from her shoulders. "Thank you, Zia. Thank you so much."

"But..." Zia Rosa's voice dropped to a conspiratorial whisper, "we won't stop there." She winked, her mischievous spirit shining through. "After the deli closes, I'll help you find your way into one of those fashion houses or modeling agencies. You have the look, Isabella. Just like your papa said."

Isabella blinked in surprise. "How?"

Rosa smiled, tapping her finger against her lips in thought. "My Bruno... he's a photographer, you know. Well, at least he likes to think so," she said with a chuckle. "He took photography at school, and he can take pictures of you. We'll make a portfolio. And then... we'll deliver those photos to the agencies. Someone is bound to notice."

Tears welled in Isabella's eyes again, but this time, they were tears of gratitude and hope. "I can't believe it. Zia, you're helping me with my dream. You really think it could happen?"

Zia Rosa's smile widened. "I know it can, bambina. You have your papa's fire in you, and I'll do everything I can to make sure the world sees it too."

For the first time since leaving home, Isabella felt a glimmer of hope. She wasn't just running away anymore—she was running toward something. She had found someone who believed in her, who saw the potential that her father had always seen. The road ahead would be tough, but with Zia Rosa at her side, Isabella knew she could make it.

As the deli's smells of bread and meat filled the air, and the city's distant hum echoed outside, Isabella couldn't help but think how lucky she was. She had found not just refuge, but a place where her dreams could take root. And she wouldn't waste this chance. For the first time in a long while, she believed in herself. Just like her papa had.

Isabella settled into life in New York more easily than she had expected. The city mesmerized her—the towering buildings seemed to stretch into the heavens, and the bustling streets were filled with the rhythm of life that never seemed to stop. It was nothing like her quiet village in Sicily, and she often found herself staring in awe at the sea of yellow taxis, the neon lights, and the people rushing in every direction.

Thankfully, Zia Rosa lived in an Italian neighborhood, which gave Isabella a sense of home. The community welcomed her warmly; she met cousins she had only ever heard about in family stories and saw neighbors who had once known her parents, before they'd decided to stay behind in Sicily while the rest of the family immigrated. Every day, Isabella worked hard at the deli, her hands busy but her mind often drifting toward her dreams. She loved working with Zia, but she was always thinking of the modeling agencies. As promised, Zia Rosa helped her send her photos to agencies across the city. Months passed, but she didn't hear anything back.

At first, the waiting was hard, but Isabella soon found herself distracted by Marco, a handsome Italian-American man about four years older than her. He came into the deli often, always bringing her gifts—expensive perfumes, silk scarves, jewelry—things that made her feel special. Marco had that classic Italian movie star look with his dark, slicked-back hair, a strong jawline, and charming smile. Isabella was instantly taken with him, mesmerized by the way he made her feel like the most important girl in the world.

Zia Rosa, however, was not charmed by Marco. She often warned Isabella to stay away from him. "That boy is bad news," Rosa would mutter whenever Marco left the deli, shaking her head. But Isabella, naive and captivated by Marco's allure, refused to listen. She would sneak out at night to see him, lying to Zia about where she was going. Their romance blossomed quickly. He took her to glamorous places—old movie theaters, nightclubs, restaurants where the waiters knew his name. He told people he was teaching her English, but their nights out left her exhausted. She began showing up to the deli late, dragging herself through her shifts, her energy drained from too many late nights. Zia Rosa's worry grew.

One day, after Isabella came home late again, Zia Rosa confronted her. "Isabella," she said sternly, "you're losing focus. You came here to follow your dreams, not to throw them away for some man who only cares about your looks. Marco is no good for you."

Isabella's heart sank. She loved Marco, or at least she thought she did. She couldn't believe that Zia Rosa was saying these things. Devastated, she packed a small bag and ran off to stay with Marco. She continued working at the deli but grew distant from her aunt, her heart torn between her ambitions and her romance. Zia's words haunted her, but she couldn't bring herself to believe that Marco, her charming, glamorous boyfriend, could be the selfish, dangerous man Rosa implied.

Months passed in a haze of parties and late nights, but soon Isabella began to feel different. She grew nauseous in the mornings, barely making it through her shifts without running to the bathroom. Her body felt heavier, more tired than usual. She told herself it was just stress or maybe exhaustion from her lifestyle, but the truth was undeniable. One night, after feeling particularly unwell, she made an appointment with a doctor, asking Marco to come with her. That day, at only 16 years old, Isabella's world came crashing down around her. The doctor confirmed what she feared—she was pregnant. Isabella was horrified, unable to comprehend the news. Marco held her hand, assuring her that everything would be fine. He was excited, promising that they would get married and that he would take care of her and the baby. But Isabella couldn't shake the feeling that her dreams had slipped away from her grasp. She had come to New York to build a better life, to be someone different, and now it felt like all of that was gone.

A week later, while working at the deli, Zia Rosa stormed over to Isabella and slammed a newspaper down on the counter in front of her. "Look at this," Zia said, her voice tight with anger.

The headline read: **"Mob Member Finally Jailed."** And there, in a grainy black-and-white photograph, was Marco.

Isabella's heart stopped. She quickly scanned the article, her hands trembling as she read. Marco had been arrested the previous night. The authorities had been tracking him for months, and his list of crimes was horrifying—drug trafficking, robbery, and possibly even ties to mob killings. The article mentioned that he was likely to face a life sentence in prison.

Zia Rosa, not knowing Isabella was pregnant, let out a sigh of relief. "Thank goodness he's gone," she muttered. "You're better off without him. I told you he was trouble, Isabella. I told you."

Isabella didn't hear her. Her vision blurred, and her legs gave way beneath her. She collapsed to the floor, sobbing uncontrollably. Marco—her Marco, the man she had fallen in love with—had been living a lie. And now, she was left alone, pregnant, her dreams shattered beyond repair.

10

Angela woke up with a newfound sense of excitement coursing through her veins. Today, she was finally free to leave the house, no longer grounded, and she couldn't wait to be reunited with her friends. She jumped out of bed, throwing on her sneakers and grabbing her bag, hardly pausing as she ran downstairs. Her parents were deep in conversation at the breakfast table, barely noticing her as she dashed past them.

With a final glance over her shoulder, Angela slipped out of the front door, not giving her mother a chance to call her back. Her heart pounded with exhilaration as she mounted her bike and took off down the long, winding road leading to the beach, feeling the fresh morning air on her face.

She arrived at the beach cafe where her friends were already gathered, preparing for the evening's BBQ. The cafe belonged to Sophie's parents, and they were generous enough to let the group use it to do all the prep work. Angela was greeted with smiles and waves, everyone excited to see her again.

"Ella!" Jay called out, his voice full of playful warmth. "Sophie's Father should give you a job after this. You're a natural!"

Angela laughed as Sophie gave her a quick tour of the kitchen, showing her how to marinate the meats and prepare the ingredients. For the first time in a while, Angela felt like she belonged, immersed in something that wasn't superficial or staged for appearance's sake. It was simple but it was such fun.

As the day wore on and the BBQ preparations were nearly done, Angela and Jay decided to take a break. They walked down to the beach and sat on the soft sand, the sound of gentle waves lapping the shore as the afternoon sun began to dip lower in the sky.

Jay turned to her, concern evident in his eyes. "So, you doing okay after being grounded? What happened with your mom?"

Angela sighed, fidgeting awkwardly. "It's just... she's so cold, you know? Sometimes it feels like she doesn't even care. It's like I don't matter to her at all. I just don't get it."

Jay nodded in understanding, leaning back on his hands as he stared out at the ocean. "Yeah, it's hard when your parents act like that. When my father left, he never wanted anything to do with me. It hurts, but I've learned it's their problem, not ours."

Angela looked at him, grateful for his words. Jay always knew how to make her feel better, and today was no different.

"You'll meet people who care about you," Jay continued, his voice gentle. "Real people who actually want to be in your life. It makes all the difference. My mom's new boyfriend—he's been amazing. At first, I didn't know what to think, but he's been playing football with me, teaching me how to surf... He's even taking me camping for a few days. For the first time, it feels like I've got a proper family."

Angela smiled, happy for him, but also feeling a pang of envy. "That's really great, Jay. I'm glad you have that. Maybe one day I'll feel that too."

"You will," Jay said with confidence, looking at her with his deep, understanding eyes. "When you have your own family, a husband, and kids... you'll see."

Angela blushed, the thought of a future that felt so far away suddenly becoming something she longed for. She studied Jay's face—the kind smile, the warmth in his eyes, the way he always knew how to say just the right thing.

At that moment, she realized something she hadn't quite been ready to admit. She was only fifteen, but in her heart, she knew that one day, she wanted to marry someone like Jay—kind, attentive, and full of understanding. The kind of person who would never make her feel invisible or unloved. The kind of person who made her feel like she mattered.

As the sun began to set, they sat in comfortable silence, both of them thinking about the futures they hoped to build, together or apart.

Tomorrow, Jay would be off on his camping trip with his mother and her boyfriend, but Angela knew this wasn't the last time they'd share moments like this. And as she headed back to the group, feeling lighter than she had in days, she smiled to herself, knowing that she had found something truly special in this summer, in this town, and in Jay.

11

Angela had the time of her life at the **BBQ**. Surrounded by her new friends, she danced barefoot on the sand, the bonfire lighting up their faces as music played in the background. The night was perfect—the kind of evening that only summer could create. They swam in the ocean, played games, and sang songs by the fire. Jay was always close by, his presence a constant source of comfort. Every time his leg brushed against hers, a jolt of electricity ran through her. She felt like she belonged there, in that instant, with these people.

As the sun set and the temperature dipped, Jay took off his jumper and handed it to her. "Here, you look cold."

Angela pulled it over her head, inhaling the faint scent of him that lingered on the fabric. It smelled like salt and summer, and it wrapped her in a warmth that went beyond the material. As they sang and danced around the fire, Jay held her hands, his touch lingering longer than usual. At times, she thought he might kiss her, but he never did. The tension between them was undeniable, but he seemed content just being by her side.

When the night came to a bittersweet end, Angela felt a pang of sadness. She didn't want it to be over, and worse, she knew she wouldn't be seeing Jay for a few days. He was going camping with his mother and her boyfriend. Just before she left, Jay pulled out a small piece of paper and handed it to her.

"In case you need it," he said, his dark eyes meeting hers.

Angela unfolded the paper, revealing his house phone number scrawled in messy handwriting. She smiled, touched by the gesture. After what happened before, when they couldn't reach each other, he wanted to make sure they never lost contact again.

"Thank you," she whispered, slipping the note into her pocket and feeling the warmth of his thoughtfulness.

As she rode her bike home, Angela was filled with a mix of emotions—joy, excitement, and a deep sense of belonging she hadn't felt in years. The night had been perfect, but something was bothering her at the back of her mind, a sinking feeling she couldn't shake. When she arrived back at the house, she froze.

Her mother was standing on the front steps, the family limo parked outside, and the chauffeur packing up the last of the suitcases. Angela's heart plummeted.

"What's going on?" she asked, panic rising in her chest.

Her mother turned to her, her face cold and unreadable.

"We're leaving. Going back to the city."

"No!" Angela screamed, her voice cracking with desperation. "We still have a week left! Please, Mother, no!"

Isabella remained silent, her expression unmoved by her daughter's pleas. Angela ran to her, dropping to the ground and grabbing her mother's legs, sobbing as she begged to stay. Through tear-filled eyes, she saw her father watching from the dining room window, his face as distant and cold as ever. It felt like no one cared about how much she had grown attached to this place, to these people.

"We're going home," Isabella said, her tone final. "Your father has work. Your sisters will finish up the social events and return in a few days."

The limo doors opened, and Angela was forced inside. She cried the entire way back to the city, watching the world she had come to love, disappear through the tinted windows. The streets of New York, once familiar and comforting, now felt cold and unwelcoming. She felt trapped, her sense of freedom ripped away from her.

Clinging to Jay's note, Angela read it over and over as if it were the only thing tethering her to her summer, to him. *Hey Ella, here's my number so we are never separated again. Jay.* He had even signed it with a kiss, and that tiny detail made her heart ache.

But she couldn't call him—not tonight. By now, he'd be asleep, and in the morning, he'd be off on his camping trip.

She was desperate to hear his voice, but she knew she had to wait. At least now she had his number, a piece of him that she could hold onto until they were reunited.

Later that night, as Angela lay curled up in her bed, her mother came into her room. Isabella's face was stern, though her eyes softened just a little.

"Angela," her mother began, "I don't want you getting mixed up with the wrong people. You'll thank me one day."

Angela looked up at her, tears pooling in her eyes, but she didn't respond. She had no words for the emptiness that chipped away at her from the inside. She watched as her mother shut the door, leaving her alone with her thoughts.

She cried herself to sleep that night, the note from Jay clutched tightly in her hand, knowing that summer—her freedom, her friends, and the boy she was falling for—was slipping away from her faster than she could grasp.

12

The next few days passed in a blur for Angela. The walls of her family's grand apartment seemed to close in on her as she waited for the right moment to call Jay. The slip of paper with his number never left her side, tucked safely in her pocket or under her pillow at night. She rehearsed what she'd say in her head, but every time she picked up the phone, she lost her nerve.

Finally, she could wait no longer. Her heart raced as she dialed the number, each ring stretching into what felt like an eternity. Then, a warm and kind female voice answered, immediately making Angela feel at ease.

"Is this Ella?" Jay's mother asked kindly. "Jay's been waiting for your call. Let me get him."

Seconds later, she heard Jay's sleepy but excited voice on the line. "Ella?"

Hearing him say her name made her feel lighter. "Jay!" she said, her voice shaky but filled with relief. "I've missed you. How was the trip?"

Jay let out a small laugh. "I've missed you too. I was worried when the gang said they hadn't seen you since I left. What happened?"

Angela told him everything—how her mother had made them pack up early, cutting their summer short, and how devastated she'd been to leave without saying goodbye. She confessed how she cried the whole way back to the city and how trapped she felt in her family's apartment.

Jay listened quietly, then said, "I'm sorry, Ella. I wish you could've stayed."

"I'll be back next summer," she promised, her voice filled with determination. "And maybe we can call each other until then?"

"I'd like that," Jay replied, his tone softening. The smile in his voice was clear, and it made Angela's heart swell.

They talked for what felt like hours, though the time flew by in a blur. Jay told Angela all about his camping trip with his mom and her boyfriend. "We went kayaking, made dens in the woods, even tried windsurfing—though I wasn't great at it." He laughed. "But it was amazing. Her boyfriend, he's... well, I think he wants to stick around. He told me he wants to look after my mom, and he asked for my blessing."

Angela was over the moon for Jay. She could hear the joy in his voice, and it warmed her to know that, after all the struggles he and his mother had been through, they were finally finding happiness. "That's incredible, Jay. You deserve that—a real family."

"Thanks, Ella," Jay said, his voice softening. "I hope so. I've never seen my mom so happy, and honestly, it feels good to have someone who cares about us both."

They spent the rest of the call talking about the next summer, making plans and dreaming up new adventures. Jay told her he planned on getting a job at Sophie's café. "You should work there too," he suggested. "It'll be fun."

Angela smiled at the thought, her heart lifting as she imagined spending every day with Jay and the gang. "I'd love that," she said. But the minute she hung up, a wave of panic washed over her.

What if my mother doesn't let me go back next summer?
The thought hit her hard, and she felt her chest tighten. She knew her mother had her own plans, and they rarely included considering Angela's happiness. But she quickly pushed the worry to the back of her mind, refusing to let it ruin the joy of right now.

That night, as she lay in bed, she clutched Jay's number in her hand, a smile playing on her lips. Even though she was miles away from the Hamptons, she felt closer to him than ever. Her thoughts were filled with the next summer, the adventures they'd have, and the hope that Jay would call again soon.

13

As the weeks turned into months, Angela and Jay's phone conversations became the highlight of her life. Each time they spoke, they grew closer, their banter turning flirtier with each call. Jay would tease her about the "special things" he had planned for their reunion, hinting at secret spots on the beach and late-night adventures that made Angela's heart race with anticipation. He even managed to secure jobs for both of them at Sophie's café, and they would laugh about how much fun it would be to spend every day together when summer came around again.

However, at home, things were less certain. Angela had tried, repeatedly, to bring up the summer plans with her mother. But Isabella always gave vague answers, brushing her off with comments like, "We'll see" or "Perhaps we'll visit

France this year. Your sister and Pierre are waiting for us." The thought of not going back to the Hamptons filled Angela with dread, but she clung to her weekly phone calls with Jay. It was the one thing keeping her spirits high as the monotony of schoolwork and after-school activities consumed her days. Her mother made sure her schedule was packed tight, leaving little room for Angela to even think about the summer.

Then, one spring morning, everything changed.

Angela and her sisters were having breakfast, discussing the latest gossip from their social circles, when their mother burst into the room, practically vibrating with excitement. Her eyes were wide, her hands flailing as she struggled to get the words out.

"You won't believe it!" Isabella shrieked, her voice a mixture of shock and exhilaration. "We've been invited to the biggest Hamptons gala in history! And it's all because of him."

The girls exchanged confused glances. "Who's 'him'?" Bianca asked, clearly less interested than their mother.

"The Prince!" Isabella nearly shouted. "An English prince is vacationing in the Hamptons this summer, and they're throwing a massive gala in his honor at the end of the season! Can you believe it? A prince, right here!"

Angela's heart stopped for a moment. The Hamptons? Gala? End of summer? That means we'll be there all summer long! Her pulse quickened as the realization sank in. Not only would they be back in the Hamptons, but they would be there until the very end of summer, just like she had dreamed.

Meanwhile, Isabella had already shifted into her usual social-climbing mode. She turned her attention to Camilla, who was only a couple of years younger than the prince. "Camilla, darling, this is **your** moment! We need to get you noticed by the prince. This is your chance to marry into British royalty!"

Camilla, who had always enjoyed the attention, looked intrigued, though not entirely surprised by their mother's dramatic reaction. Isabella was already planning grand shopping trips to update Camilla's wardrobe with designer dresses "fit for a princess."

"We need to be at every party, every event the prince attends," Isabella went on, her voice filled with determination. "We'll host dinners, we'll network with all the right people. We'll make sure that by the end of summer, he notices you."

Angela felt an odd sense of relief wash over her. If her mother's focus was entirely on Camilla and the prince, that meant she could fly under the radar for the entire summer. She could sneak off to the beach, spend time with Jay and her friends, and take the job at the café without anyone caring where she was. It would be perfect.

Angela quickly excused herself from the table, her excitement bubbling over as she ran to her room and grabbed the phone. Her fingers trembled as she dialed Jay's number, the anticipation of telling him the good news making her heart race.

When Jay picked up, his familiar voice was all she needed to feel like everything was going to be okay.

"Hey, Ella," he said, and she could hear the smile in his voice.

"Jay! You're not going to believe this," Angela exclaimed breathlessly. "We're coming back to the Hamptons this summer! The whole summer. And not just that, but we're staying till the end!"

"What? That's amazing!" Jay replied, sounding just as excited as she felt. "What changed?"

Angela grinned, her voice filled with amusement. "There's a prince coming to the Hamptons this year, and my mother's obsessed with the idea of my sister catching his eye. She's already planning for us to host all these parties and events to get noticed."

Jay laughed. "Well, that sounds like a perfect distraction for you."

"Exactly!" Angela said, her voice practically bouncing with joy. "No one will care where I am. I can take the job at Sophie's café, and we can hang out every day without anyone bothering us!"

"That's perfect," Jay said warmly. "It's gonna be the best summer ever, Ella. I can't wait."

Neither could Angela. All the worries she'd been carrying about next summer melted away as she imagined the months ahead. Jay had a way of making everything feel lighter, brighter. And now, she could finally see the light at the end of the tunnel. Summer in the Hamptons, with Jay by her side.

It was all she'd ever wanted.

For the rest of the day, Angela floated on air, already imagining the countless beach days and late-night bonfires. The thought of disappearing into the backdrop while her family fawned over the prince was just the icing on the cake.

Little did they know, her own summer romance was already in full bloom.

14

Zia Rosa stood frozen, her heart aching as she watched Isabella collapse onto the floor. The reality of the situation was sinking in fast—Isabella was pregnant. Rosa had feared it for weeks, noticing the subtle changes in her niece's body, but she had prayed it wasn't true. As Isabella sobbed, begging for her aunt's forgiveness, Rosa bent down, gathering her trembling niece into her arms.

"Oh no," Rosa whispered, her voice barely audible. The weight of what had happened pressed down on her chest. She had to help Isabella; there was no other choice.

"Please, Zia," Isabella pleaded, her voice thick with desperation. "Help me. I don't know what to do."

Rosa hugged her tightly, reassuring her. "Shh, bambina. We'll figure something out. Don't worry. I won't let this ruin your life."

Over the next few days, Rosa wracked her brain, considering all the possibilities. Then, she came up with a plan. A few days later, she pulled Isabella aside with a mix of hope and sorrow in her eyes. "Isabella," she began, "a letter came from one of the top modeling agencies in New York. They want to meet with you."

Isabella's eyes lit up, a glimmer of her old self resurfacing for a brief second. "Really? They still want me?"

Rosa nodded. "Yes, but you'll need time to get things in order. We'll tell them you had to return to Italy for a few months due to family reasons. But first, we need to... take care of this."

Isabella's gaze dropped, the weight of her situation pressing down again. "What are you suggesting?"

Rosa took a deep breath. "You'll go to a convent. It's quiet, no one will know you're there. The nuns will take care of you until the baby is born. Then, you'll give the child up for adoption to a family who can provide for the baby."

Isabella flinched at the word "adoption," her heart aching. "But Zia... how can I do that? What if I want to keep it?"

Rosa's eyes softened as she reached for Isabella's hand. "You're 16, Isabella. You have nothing right now. No money, no career. You're not ready for this. We'll delay the meeting with the agency, and when you're back, you'll start fresh. You're young, bella, you'll bounce back. No one has to know."

Isabella's heart twisted with pain, but deep down, she knew Rosa was right. She wasn't ready to be a mother. "Okay," she whispered, tears spilling down her cheeks. "I'll do it."

The following day, Rosa helped Isabella pack her things and took her to the small convent on the outskirts of the city. The building was old and worn, with peeling paint and small, narrow windows. When they arrived, they were greeted by a group of kind, gentle nuns, one of whom, Sister Augusta, placed a comforting hand on Isabella's shoulder.

"We will take care of you, dear child," Sister Augusta said softly, her voice soothing.

Over the next three months, Isabella hid away at the convent, helping with chores around the church—cooking, cleaning, and preparing for services. She stayed out of sight, hidden from the community, as Rosa had told everyone that Isabella had returned to Sicily. The lie worked; no one suspected a thing.

Then, the day came. Isabella went into labor in the early hours of the morning. It was an agonizing process, but by late afternoon, she gave birth to a beautiful baby boy. As the nurse placed him in her arms, Isabella stared down at his tiny face, overwhelmed by emotion. His delicate rosebud lips, his little dark eyes—**Marco's eyes**—stared back at her, and for a moment, she felt a surge of love so strong, it nearly made her arms give way.

He was perfect. How could she give him up- how could she lose him?

As she held him close, breathing in his soft scent, her mind raced with doubts. Could she do this? Could she let him go? He was her son. He was a part of her. Maybe she could make it work, somehow.

But as those thoughts circled in her mind, reality sank in. She had nothing. No job, no home, no family who could support her as a single mother. She couldn't give him the life he deserved.

"I don't know if I can do this," Isabella whispered to Sister Augusta, her voice cracking with emotion.

Sister Augusta, who had become a mother figure to her during her time at the convent, gave her a soft, understanding smile. "You don't have to do anything you don't want to, Isabella. Remember, a child doesn't need fancy things, a child just needs love above all else."

"I love him so much," Isabella sobbed, her tears falling onto her son's tiny blanket. "But love isn't enough. He deserves more than I can give him."

She thought about the couple who were waiting for him, a couple desperate for a child after years of trying and failing. They lived in upstate New York—one was a teacher, the other a doctor. They could provide for him, offer him a stable, loving home.

Isabella's heart broke as she kissed her baby boy one last time, cradling his tiny body against hers. "I love you," she whispered, her voice trembling. "I love you so much."

With that, she handed him over to Sister Augusta, her body shivering.

Sister Augusta hesitated, holding the baby as she glanced back at Isabella, waiting for her to change her mind. But

Isabella turned her head away, unable to watch as her son was taken from her.

As Sister Augusta walked away, her footsteps echoing down the hall, Isabella felt her heart shatter. She stared at the wall, her tears falling silently, her chest heavy with grief.

Her baby boy was gone. And with him, a part of her soul.

15

As spring gave way to summer, the days in the city felt like they dragged on forever, but Angela's anticipation grew with each passing minute. Finally, the house was buzzing with excitement as her family prepared to leave for the Hamptons. This year was different—larger luggage piles, more frantic energy. Even Francesca and her husband Pierre had flown in from France to be part of the summer spectacle. The whole family was eager to experience what was being called the "summer of a lifetime."

Of course, for Angela, the reason for her excitement had nothing to do with the royal buzz surrounding the prince's impending visit. She was thrilled for an entirely different reason—Jay. Her heart raced at the thought of seeing him again, of their long-awaited reunion. She had been counting the days, replaying his voice in her head, clinging to every detail from their phone calls. The rest of the family thought she was just caught up in the excitement about the royal gala, and she let them believe it. They didn't need to know her real plans.

As they arrived at the Hamptons, they were greeted by the house staff who were already lined up and ready to receive instructions from her mother. Isabella wasted no time barking orders, making sure every detail for the summer's lavish events was taken care of. Angela barely noticed; she was already mentally checking out. As soon as the car doors opened, she dashed up to her room to change.

She had been dreaming about this day for months—her first shift at the beach café, working alongside Jay. He had promised to show her the ropes, and she couldn't wait to slip back into the life she loved. Unlike her sisters and mother, who craved attention and status, Angela wanted to blend into the quiet, carefree world she'd found with Jay and their friends.

Angela slipped on her jean shorts and a crisp white t-shirt, pulling her dark hair into a high ponytail. She glanced at herself in the mirror—simple, carefree, and ready. No fancy dresses or designer labels, just herself. She hurried down the stairs, already thinking about the drive to the café.

At 16, Angela was now old enough to drive, and she had cleverly secured permission to borrow one of the staff's cars for the summer. Of course, it wasn't her mother or father who had agreed to let her use it—it was one of the housemaids, Maria, whom Angela had known since she was a baby. Maria had always looked out for her, as did many of the staff. In fact, Angela felt more at home with them than she ever had with her own family. Unlike the cold, detached world of her parents and sisters, the staff had practically raised her. They understood her, and she was grateful for them.

As she ran through the kitchen, Maria winked at her, passing her the keys without a word. "The car's ready for you, Miss Angela," she said with a soft smile. "And don't worry, the kitchen door will be open if you need anything."

"Thanks, Maria. You're the best," Angela replied, grinning widely.

The staff always had her back, and they were happy to do it. Angela wasn't like her mother or sisters—she was kind, considerate, and treated them like people, not servants. That's why they adored her, why they always kept a watchful eye out for her, making sure she was safe. She was the quiet heartbeat of the house, the one they all hoped would be okay amidst the chaos of her family's glamorous, superficial world.

Angela slid into the car and turned on the engine, the sound giving her a rush of freedom. With one last glance at the towering mansion behind her, she drove off toward the beach café, her heart pounding with excitement.

Jay was waiting for her. This summer was going to be theirs

Angela's heart pounded as she pulled up to the café, spotting Jay through the window. He was busy, serving customers, but he looked different—his hair shorter, his physique more defined, and his skin glowing with a deep, sun-kissed tan. He looked even more perfect than she remembered, and seeing him in his element made her heart race. She couldn't believe she was finally back—back to where she felt she truly belonged.

Her nerves fluttered in her chest as she parked the car. Angela quickly checked her reflection in the mirror, smoothing her dark curls and retouching her subtle makeup. Her deep blue eyes seemed to glow, and her olive skin radiated a natural warmth, especially under the soft summer sunlight. Just as she reached for the door, she noticed movement and glanced up.

Jay was already there, standing beside her car, grinning that wide, heart-stopping grin. His eyes, however, were intense, locking onto hers as if they were the only two people in the world. Time seemed to slow down. Without a word, he opened her car door gently and took her hand, pulling her from the seat. His touch was electric, his closeness making her breath hitch.

"Hi," he whispered, his voice barely above a murmur but laced with emotion. His eyes never left hers.

Angela's voice caught in her throat, but she managed a quiet, "Hello."

Before she could say anything else, as if in some kind of surreal dream, Jay leaned in and softly kissed her. It was the kiss she had been waiting for—gentle but powerful, like a wave sweeping her off her feet. Her legs nearly gave out beneath her as his lips touched hers. The world seemed to stop. Everything else faded, except for him.

Jay pulled back, his face lighting up with a smile. "I've been waiting a whole year to do that," he said, his voice warm and playful.

Angela let out a soft, shy laugh, her heart fluttering wildly in her chest. This time, Jay kissed her again, but with more intensity, more passion. She melted into the kiss, the connection between them feeling stronger than ever.

But the magic of the moment was quickly interrupted by a chorus of cheers and laughter. Angela and Jay broke apart, turning to see their entire group of friends gathered outside the café, clapping and shouting with teasing smiles.

"About time!" one of them yelled, while others whistled and hollered in celebration.

Angela's cheeks flushed with embarrassment, but she couldn't stop grinning. Jay just shook his head, chuckling as he took her hand in his, leading her toward the café.

As they walked hand in hand into the beach café, surrounded by their friends, Angela felt lighter than she had in months. She was exactly where she wanted to be—by Jay's side, surrounded by people who cared about her. And as she glanced up at him, she knew the best was yet to come.

16

Angela adored her time working at the café. It wasn't about the money; it was the simple joy of spending her days with Jay and their friends, in a place where she felt she belonged. Sophie's parents, who ran the café, were kind and welcoming, treating Angela like part of their extended family. The small beach town had become a haven for her— a place where she could escape the stifling expectations of her family and just be herself.

    She loved talking to the locals, especially the older folk who would share stories from their youth, and she was always there to lend a sympathetic ear to the younger ones with their dramas. Angela had become a quick learner, handling the café work with ease, and her natural kindness made her popular with everyone who came through the doors.

After work, she and Jay would head out on long walks along the shore or take bike rides through the coastal roads, exploring every inch of the town. Other nights, they would meet up with their gang to have beach parties, bonfires, or even impromptu camping trips under the stars. They danced in the rain and sunbathed on the shores- life was a dream. The freedom Angela felt during these times was intoxicating, a stark contrast to her structured life back in the city.

One evening, a few weeks into the summer, after the café had closed for the night, Jay and Angela decided to take a small boat out onto the water. They paddled into the gentle waves until they were far enough from shore that the only sounds were the lapping of the water and the occasional cry of seagulls. The sky was clear, and the stars above shimmered like diamonds scattered across velvet.

Angela had never seen anything so breathtaking before. Sitting in the boat with Jay, the world felt endless, and so did the possibilities for their future.

As they floated, Jay opened up to her about his family. He told her his mother was pregnant. "I'm happy for her and her boyfriend," he said, his voice steady, though a little unsure. "He's a great guy. He's been good to both of us. But I think it's time for me to move on, to go to college. I want to give them space, you know?"

Angela nodded, her hand finding his in the darkness, giving him a reassuring squeeze.

Jay continued, his tone brightening. "I've been thinking about going to college in New York. That way, I'd be close to you. And next year, when I turn 18, maybe we could get an apartment together. We wouldn't have to worry about being separated ever again."

Angela's heart raced at the thought. Living together, just the two of them—it sounded like a dream. She shared her own hopes with him, telling him about her passion for animals and how she wanted to become a vet. She had even imagined moving to Africa someday to help endangered species.

Jay listened intently, then smiled. "That sounds amazing. You'd be an incredible vet. I could come with you, you know. Maybe I could teach over there, help the community while you're saving animals. We could make a difference together."

They laughed and joked, imagining their future lives, far from the pressures of their families, far from the expectations others had set for them. Everything felt perfect, and in that instant, under the starry sky, Angela believed that it could be. For the first time in a long while, her future didn't seem so uncertain. She had Jay by her side, and that was all she needed.

One early morning, Angela was jolted awake by the sound of her sister's frantic cries. She rubbed her eyes and opened her door, just in time to see the staff rushing upstairs. Maria shot her a quick eyeroll as she passed, and Angela couldn't help but smile despite the chaos.

Her sister Camilla had woken up with a rash all over her body, and it was apparently the end of the world. Camilla had been invited to an exclusive tea at the prince's residence, and now, it seemed, everything was falling apart. Isabella, their mother, was screaming for the doctor, her voice frantic and high-pitched.

As the staff swarmed around Camilla, Isabella turned her gaze sharply toward Angela. "You need to get ready."

"Why me?" Angela asked, confused, still standing in her doorway.

"He's expecting a Hastings girl, and a Hastings girl he will get," Isabella snapped. "Bianca is too old, and Francesca is married, so that leaves you. Now hurry up!"

Angela's face fell. "I'm not going," she said firmly. "I have plans."

Isabella's eyes flashed with fury. "You don't have a choice! You're going. I don't care about your silly plans."

Tears welled up in Angela's eyes as she turned and stormed to her room. Maria, sensing her distress, quietly followed her in and closed the door. "It's going to be okay," Maria said softly, pulling Angela into a comforting hug. Angela rested her head on Maria's shoulder.

"I'm supposed to be with Jay today. I was going to work my shift at the café, and now I'm stuck going to some stupid tea with a stuffy prince I don't care about!" Angela's voice cracked as she fought back sobs.

Maria nodded, understanding. "Don't worry, I'll head to the café and explain everything to Jay," she said gently. "You focus on getting through this. I'll make sure he knows."

Angela looked at her gratefully. "Thank you."

Later that afternoon, Angela arrived at the grand estate where the royal tea was being held. She felt completely out of place in the stiff, formal outfit her mother had chosen for her. As she and her sisters walked through the grand hallway and out onto the veranda, her heart sank. The prince and his entourage entered, and everyone stood up, bowing and curtsying. Everyone except Angela.

Isabella shot her a sharp glare, and Angela reluctantly followed suit, feeling more awkward with each passing second.

The conversation was dull, her mother rambling on about their family as if they were showpieces on display. Angela kept her distance, staring out at the sea. When the prince finally spoke to her, his eyes lingering on her, she felt trapped. He asked her a few polite questions, clearly intrigued by her beauty. But Angela's responses were short and distant.

Just as the prince was about to invite her for a walk, Camilla, fully recovered, burst onto the veranda. Her confidence and charm were impossible to ignore as she whisked the prince away, making sure he hardly noticed Angela's disappearance.

Angela felt relieved but drained as they returned home. Isabella wasted no time tearing into her. "You embarrassed us! How dare you act so distant and rude? This was our chance, and you threw it away!"

Maria was standing nearby, collecting the girls' bags. As Isabella's angry words rang in Angela's ears, she couldn't take it anymore. She ran to her room, tears streaming down her face as she threw herself onto the bed. She sobbed uncontrollably, muffling her cries into her pillow.

Minutes later, she heard a gentle knock. Maria slipped into the room, sitting down beside her. "It's okay," she whispered softly, brushing Angela's hair out of her face.

"I don't understand why they hate me so much," Angela choked out, her voice filled with hurt.

"They don't hate you," Maria said hesitantly, her expression turning serious. "They're just... hurting."

Angela's brow creased as she wiped her tears. "Hurting? What do you mean?"

Maria hesitated, her voice barely above a whisper. "I'll tell you, but you have to promise me something. You can never, ever tell anyone I told you this. If your parents find out, they'll fire me."

Angela's heart skipped a beat. She sat up, her tears forgotten as curiosity and dread swirled inside her. "I promise," she whispered back. "I'll never say a word."

Maria took a deep breath, her eyes flickering toward the door. "There's something you don't know about your family... something you need to hear."

Angela leaned in closer, her pulse quickening, knowing that whatever Maria was about to reveal would change everything.

17

A month after giving birth, Zia Rosa picked Isabella up from the convent in a yellow taxi. Just as Rosa had predicted, there was no sign that Isabella, not yet seventeen, had carried a child. She looked every bit the radiant young woman she had always been, her beauty undiminished. As they bid farewell to the nuns, Isabella hugged Sister Augusta tightly, holding back tears.

"Please, heal your broken heart, child, this is not where love ends for you- stitch those broken pieces back together." Sister Augusta said softly. "Beauty fades, but love... love is eternal."

But Isabella felt cold inside. Her heart had frozen over after everything she'd lost—her father, the love of her life, and now her baby son. It was as though the part of her capable of love had been buried beneath the weight of her pain. She nodded politely, but her mind was far away. She had no room for love anymore. Only ambition filled the void now.

After a long drive, Rosa took her to an old apartment building in Queens. It was far from the life Isabella had dreamed of.

"Why am I not going back home with you?" Isabella asked, her voice sharp with confusion as they pulled up in front of the worn building.

Rosa turned to face her niece, her eyes soft but resolute. "It's time for you to stand on your own," she said. "I've told everyone that you went back to Sicily. It's better this way—no one will ask questions."

Isabella's heart sank as she realized what this meant. She was truly alone.

"I've paid two months' rent for you," Rosa continued. "There's some cash in here." She handed Isabella an envelope. "I've set up meetings with modeling agencies. But I can't save you anymore, Isabella. It's time for you to take responsibility for your life."

Rosa embraced her tightly before getting back into the taxi. Isabella stood on the sidewalk, clutching the envelope, her face blank as Rosa disappeared into the city traffic. Alone for the first time in her life.

Later that week, Isabella took out the designer dress that Marco had given her all those months ago. She put it on carefully, as though it were armor. She did her hair and makeup meticulously, every stroke of eyeliner and curl of hair designed to hide the loneliness gnawing at her insides. She felt hollow—like a shell of the person she had once been. But no one could ever know.

From that day on, she was no longer just Isabella. She was Isabella Verona, a new identity born from her pain and determination. No one could hurt her again. She would make sure of it.

As she stepped out of the taxi at the agency, heads turned. She looked like she belonged on the cover of a magazine—her confidence masked every inch of insecurity hiding beneath her skin. Men and women alike stared as she walked into the building, her posture perfect, her every movement deliberate.

She approached the receptionist, flashing a dazzling smile. "I have an appointment with the director," she said, her voice steady and assertive. "Tell him Isabella Verona is here to see him."

And in that moment, the past seemed to fall away. She was no longer the girl who had lost everything. She was Isabella Verona, and the world was about to know her name.

18

Maria hesitated, holding her breath as though she regretted what she was about to say. But Angela deserved to know the truth. Her two older sisters had already discovered the secret through the whispers of New York's social circuit. It was only a matter of time until Angela heard it, and Maria wanted her to learn it from someone who loved her.

"Your Father," Maria began softly, "he never hid the fact that he wanted a boy. A son to carry on the family business, to do all the things fathers do with their sons. They had your three sisters, and though they seemed happy, Daniel kept pressuring your mother for another child—a boy this time. I could see how hard it was on Isabella."

Angela's chest tightened as she listened. She had never heard this story before.

"After years of trying," Maria continued, "your mother finally got pregnant again. They were over the moon. They rushed to the doctor for the gender reveal, and when they heard they were having a boy, it was like a dream come true. I've never seen them so united."

Angela could picture it—the perfect couple, finally expecting their long-awaited son.

"They went all out," Maria said, shaking her head. "Designers were brought in to create the most beautiful nursery. They announced it in the papers, held an extravagant baby shower. The world was ready to welcome little Angelo, named after your grandfather. Everything was baby blue—clothes specially made, the whole city buzzing with excitement."

Maria's eyes darkened as she recalled the past. "But then one night, Isabella woke up in terrible pain. She was rushed to the hospital, and things got serious quickly. Isabella nearly died, but they saved her—and they saved the baby."

Angela's heart raced. This was where it all went wrong. She could feel it.

"But when the baby was born," Maria said, her voice lowering, "it wasn't a boy. It was a girl. It was you."

Angela felt as though the floor had dropped from under her.

"Your parents were in shock," Maria said, her eyes filling with sorrow. "Not only were they devastated by the gender mistake, but because of the complications, the doctors told Isabella she could never have children again. They had to face the world, embarrassed after announcing the birth of a boy to everyone. Your mother was sent to the Hamptons to recover, and she was too weak to take care of you. So we—the staff—stepped in. We took care of you, and you were such a beautiful, easy baby. You brought so much joy into our lives."

Angela's mind swirled. All these years, she had sensed something was wrong, but she had never known why. Now, everything was falling into place. The distant parents, the feelings of never being enough—it all made sense.

"But your mother," Maria continued, her voice thick with emotion, "she wasn't the same after that. She kept talking about a lost baby boy, as if she believed he was still there. Sometimes we wondered if she thought you were a boy. She had a breakdown, I think. And your father... he threw himself into his work. He stopped talking, stopped spending time with the family. He didn't know how to handle it."

Angela felt nauseous. All her life, she had felt like something was her fault, like she was missing some crucial piece that would make her worthy of her parents' love. But now she knew the truth. It wasn't her. It had never been her.

Maria reached out, taking Angela's hand. "None of this was your fault," she said firmly. "You are a wonderful, kind person. You brought so much love into our lives, even if your parents couldn't see it. They were lost in their own pain, but that doesn't mean you did anything wrong. We all felt blessed to watch over you, to see the person you've become."

Angela's heart ached. All these years, it had been Maria and the other staff who raised her, who gave her the love she craved. She hadn't belonged in the artificial world of wealth and status because she had been brought up by people who cared for her, people who loved her deeply.

Maria pulled her into a tight embrace, both of them sobbing together. "Your parents don't know how lucky they are," Maria whispered. "Not because of their money or their status, but because of you. One day they might see it. But don't wait for that, and don't let it define you. Go out into the world, love yourself, and others will love you too, Angela Hastings. You have so much to offer. And it sounds like you already are at the café. Sophie and the others are always telling me how wonderful you are. I felt so proud."

She kissed Angela's forehead gently before leaving the room, closing the door softly behind her. Angela remained on the bed, her tears of sorrow mixing with an unexpected sense of relief.

All this time, she had been carrying the weight of her parents' disappointment, but now she understood—it wasn't her burden to bear. They had failed her, not the other way around.

She lay there for a minute longer, absorbing everything she had just learned. Her past would always be a part of her, but it didn't have to define her future.

Angela knew she would find her own way—with or without her parents.

The next morning, Jay was waiting on the beach outside Angela's house, a deep frown etched across his face. Angela spotted him from her bedroom window and felt a wave of relief wash over her. She hurried downstairs and ran out to meet him. As soon as they embraced, the tension melted away.

"I was worried," Jay said softly. "You didn't show up to work yesterday."

They walked along the shoreline, the early morning sun casting a golden glow over the water. As the waves lapped at their feet, Angela told him everything—about the prince, the disaster of the tea, and the shocking revelation from Maria. Jay listened in stunned silence, his face perplexed in disbelief.

"Your parents... I can't believe it," he finally said. "But Ella, none of that changes who you are. You're amazing, and the people who matter? They see that."

He squeezed her hand, reassuring her in the way only he could. His words were warm and comforting, like the soft summer breeze. They wandered for hours, lost in conversation, before Jay turned to her with a mischievous grin.

"How about we go camping tonight? Just us. It's our day off."

Angela smiled, the idea of escaping with Jay was too perfect to resist. She quickly snuck home, packed her things, and let Maria know where she'd be. By late afternoon, they were off to set up camp in the dunes, hidden away from the world. They spent the evening laughing, talking, playing silly games, and eventually, fell asleep under the stars. Angela felt free. With Jay, she wasn't the girl who didn't live up to her family's expectations. She was everything he ever wanted, and that made her feel whole.

The next morning, groggy and covered in sand, they returned to the café for their shift. Sophie, noticing their disheveled state, let Angela use her bedroom to freshen up.

After a quick shower, Angela was back in the kitchen, ready to start the day.

But just as she was about to leave the kitchen, something caught her eye—a tall, impeccably dressed woman with dark hair had just entered the café. Angela froze. It was her mother.

Isabella Hastings stood out in the quaint café like a diamond in the rough. The entire room seemed to turn and stare at the woman who clearly didn't belong. Angela's heart dropped into her stomach.

Jay, noticing the look of panic on Angela's face through the kitchen door window, rushed to her side. "What is she doing here?" Angela whispered, her voice shaking.

"She can't see me here, Jay. She'll ruin everything. But I can't escape—there's no way out!"

Jay thought fast, grabbing her hand. "There's an old hatch in the kitchen. Sophie and I used to play hide-and-seek in it as kids. It leads out back—no one will see you. Go, I'll cover for you."

Without wasting another second, Jay helped Angela squeeze through the small, disused garbage chute. She hurried to her car, her heart racing, desperate to avoid a confrontation.

Meanwhile, Jay stepped out from the kitchen and walked straight up to Isabella, who was scanning the café like a hawk hunting prey. Her cold eyes fell on him immediately.

"Can I help you, ma'am?" he asked, keeping his voice steady.

Isabella's eyes narrowed, looking Jay up and down with clear disdain. "You must be Jay. I saw you at my house yesterday. Now, where is my daughter? What have you done with her?"

Jay kept his cool. "She left here a while ago. Should be home by now."

Isabella scoffed, stepping closer, her voice low but sharp. "Stay away from my daughter. You don't belong in her life. You're a café worker, leading her astray. My daughter has a bright future ahead of her—one you can never be a part of. She's from a world you'll never understand."

Jay couldn't help but laugh, shaking his head. "With all due respect, you don't even know her. She's never been happy—not until she met me. You have a wonderful daughter, but I wish you could see that. Now, if you're not going to order anything, I think you should leave."

For a moment, the café was dead silent, all eyes on Isabella. She glanced around, clearly aware of the growing attention. With an awkward shift, she slipped her sunglasses on and hurried out, her heels clicking sharply against the floor. The door swung shut behind her, and she drove off in her luxury car, disappearing into the distance.

Jay stood there for a while, feeling the weight of what had just happened. His heart ached for his Ella. He had sensed the coldness she had spoken of, but seeing it firsthand—it was worse than he imagined.

As the café returned to its usual hum of chatter, Jay couldn't shake the thought of how Angela had turned out so kind, so real, despite being raised by a mother like Isabella Hastings.

19

Isabella's rise to stardom came like a tidal wave, unstoppable and overwhelming. Over the next month, her life became a whirlwind of meetings with the most prestigious modeling agencies in New York City. It seemed everyone wanted a piece of her. Offers flooded in—luxury apartments, high-paying contracts, the kind of money she'd only dreamed of. For Isabella, it felt like she had finally made it. She no longer had to beg or scrape by; the world was at her feet.

After careful consideration, she signed with an agency that promised her the lifestyle she craved. They offered her a penthouse in the heart of Manhattan, an exclusive wardrobe, and more money than she'd ever thought possible. Before long, her face was plastered across billboards, her name lighting up runways from New York to Paris. Every designer clamored to have her wear their creations, and her schedule became a blur of photoshoots, fashion weeks, and international travel.

No one knew the truth about her past—the 16-year-old girl who had been abandoned, pregnant, and alone. To the world, she was Isabella Verona, a dazzling new icon who seemed to appear out of nowhere. She was seen with Hollywood stars, photographed at glittering parties, and constantly linked to the most eligible bachelors in the tabloids. Boyfriends came and went, each more handsome and wealthy than the last. Isabella was living the dream her father had once promised her—a life of luxury, power, and admiration.

Years went by, but despite her success, Isabella knew her time in the spotlight was fleeting. The modeling world was brutal, and she had seen how quickly young, beautiful faces were replaced by even younger ones. She couldn't rely on looks alone forever. By 25, she would be considered old, and then what? She had become used to the attention, the glamour, the power, and she wasn't about to let it slip through her fingers.

So, when her friend Silvia mentioned an upcoming party hosted by the Hastings, one of New York's most powerful families, Isabella's interest piqued. George Hastings, the patriarch of the family, was known for his immense wealth and influence. But more importantly, he had a son—Daniel Hastings—who was being groomed to take over the family empire. Daniel was around Isabella's age, and according to Silvia, he was handsome, smart, and wealthy beyond imagination. He was the kind of man Isabella had been waiting for.

At the party, Silvia introduced her to Daniel. Tall and composed, he exuded an air of confidence and calm that made him stand out from the crowd of sycophants. Isabella, as always, was prepared to dazzle him. She knew everything about him thanks to Silvia—the charities he cared about, his passion for animal rights, and his commitment to ethical fashion. She was confident that she could win him over as she had with countless others.

But to her surprise, Daniel wasn't immediately captivated by her beauty. While he was polite, he seemed disinterested, his attention still focused on his long-term girlfriend, Annabel—a quiet, petite woman with a plain look who didn't say much. Despite Annabel's reserved demeanor, Daniel seemed genuinely devoted to her, which threw Isabella off her game. Men always fell for her, and yet Daniel remained unmoved.

Unfazed, Isabella turned up the charm. She strategically brought up topics she knew would intrigue him, like his work banning fur in the fashion industry. When she suggested organizing a cruelty-free fashion show to support his cause, Daniel finally took notice. He was passionate about ending the use of animal fur in fashion, and with Isabella's platform as a model, it seemed like a perfect match. Together, they began working on the event, and Isabella saw it as her way in.

Despite her best efforts, however, Daniel remained loyal to Annabel. His father, George, adored Isabella and constantly pushed Daniel to take her out, but Daniel was stubborn. He loved Annabel and had been planning to propose to her. Isabella's frustration grew. She had never had to work this hard to win a man's attention before.

Then, one afternoon during one of their meetings, Daniel walked in looking distraught, like the weight of the world had suddenly crashed down on him. He excused himself to speak privately with his father, but Isabella, ever the opportunist, couldn't resist eavesdropping.

From behind the door, she overheard everything. Daniel's voice was filled with despair as he told his father about Annabel. They had been trying for years to have a baby, but after endless tests and doctor's visits, they had received devastating news—Annabel couldn't have children. Heartbroken, she had packed her bags and left him, disappearing without a word.

"I love her, Father," Daniel said, his voice breaking. "I don't care about having children. I just want to be with her."

George, however, was unmoved. Cold and pragmatic, he told Daniel that it was for the best. "You need a son, Daniel. Someone to carry on the Hastings name, to inherit everything I've worked for. If you can't do that, you'll lose your place in this family and your inheritance."

Daniel emerged from the conversation looking shattered, torn between his love for Annabel and the crushing weight of his family's expectations. But for Isabella, this was the opening she had been waiting for. She knew that now was her chance. Daniel needed a wife, and she was determined to be that woman—the one who would secure her place in the Hastings empire and ensure her future as Isabella Hastings.

She would be his salvation, and by the end of the year, she vowed, the Hastings name would be hers.

20

The summer had gone by in what felt like the blink of an eye. Angela couldn't believe it was nearly over. The excitement surrounding the prince's visit had given way to a strange sense of deflation, especially after a shocking headline broke in one of the celebrity magazines: the prince had secretly been dating an English heiress the whole time. The news sent shockwaves through the family, particularly Isabella, who was outraged that all the time, energy, and careful plotting had been wasted. Camilla, however, took the brunt of it—devastated by the revelation. She had ended her long-term relationship with Bradley in a gamble to win the prince's heart, and now she was left heartbroken and humiliated.

The drive back to New York was tense and silent, a stark contrast to the vibrant energy the family had when they first arrived in the Hamptons. Everyone was lost in their own thoughts, brooding over the summer that had begun with so much promise but had ended in disappointment. For Angela, the sadness came from a different place entirely. She hated leaving Jay behind once again, especially after the incredible summer they had shared. Saying goodbye to him was like pulling apart the threads that had stitched her heart together over the past few months.

On their last night together, Angela and Jay stayed up until dawn, talking, laughing, and kissing under the stars. The more the sun inched toward the horizon, the heavier Angela's heart felt. She dreaded the return to her reality, where her sisters bickered and schemed, and her parents barely noticed her. Worst of all, she knew she would miss out on the everyday moments—the way Jay and their friends would go about their school days, hanging out, laughing, and having fun without her. That, more than anything, hurt.

"I'll visit when I tour colleges," Jay promised, his voice gentle but reassuring. Angela smiled at him, trying to hold on to that flicker of hope.

She wished him luck with the new baby his mum was expecting. Jay's face lit up with excitement, and Angela couldn't help but feel a pang of jealousy, even though she was genuinely happy for him. His mother's boyfriend had moved them into a big house with a pool, and for the first time in Jay's life, he had his own room. It was a stark contrast to the sofa bed he'd been sleeping on for years. He told her about how he was helping with the nursery, how things finally felt like a real family, and Angela could see how much it meant to him.

As much as Angela was thrilled for him, part of her couldn't help but feel that ache—the longing for a family like his, where love and togetherness filled the gaps that money and status couldn't touch. But she didn't dwell on it. Jay's happiness was what mattered most, and the thought of him finally having what he had always deserved made her smile.

"I'll be back next summer," Angela said softly as they embraced, the warmth of his arms a comfort she didn't want to leave behind.

"When you come, we'll throw the biggest 18th birthday pool party," Jay said, already planning it in his head. "All my friends, music, the works. You'll love it."

Angela laughed, imagining the scene, and nodded. "I can't wait." She knew it would be a long winter filled with cold, lonely nights, but she also knew that waiting for next summer—waiting for Jay—would be worth it.

Before she left, Jay gave her one last, lingering hug. "Keep being kind, and true to yourself," he whispered against her hair. "My Ella Bella."

The words stayed with her as she drove away, the Hamptons fading in the rearview mirror, the promise of another summer holding her heart steady against the long, cold wait ahead.

21

Angela fell back into her routine as if she'd never left. The whirlwind of her summer days with Jay had diminished into the background, replaced by school, family, and the busy hum of life in New York. But this year felt different. The weekly conversations with Jay from the previous summer had transformed into daily calls, solidifying their new status as boyfriend and girlfriend. Every free second she had, Angela would lock herself in her room, phone in hand, planning with Jay—discussing his 18th birthday pool party, his college applications, and dreaming about their future together. Their talks brought her a sense of stability and joy that filled the quiet gaps left by her family.

As the months passed, Angela noticed her parents even less than before. Her father seemed to have all but disappeared, showing up occasionally but always with a distant air, as if he were more of a shadow than a presence in her life. Her mother, on the other hand, had grown stranger by the day. Isabella, once so composed, now appeared jittery and distracted. Whenever they went out together, Isabella constantly glanced over her shoulder as if someone might be following them. She was more aloof than usual, often mumbling to herself or fidgeting nervously.

Angela's sisters had laughed it off, blaming her mother's odd behavior on "hormones," but Angela wasn't so sure. It seemed deeper than that—like Isabella was haunted by something no one else could see. With all her sisters now moved out and busy with their own lives, the apartment felt unusually quiet, like it was shrinking. Yet Angela didn't mind. If anything, she was more at peace with her time spent alone. With Jay, Maria, and a few others who genuinely cared about her, she felt lighter. The burden of her parents' indifference had been lifted ever since she learned the truth about her birth, and oddly enough, she now felt pity for them.

Had her parents ever really been happy? Angela doubted it. She knew bits and pieces about her mother's past in Sicily and her father's strict upbringing, but nothing beyond what was shared in passing. They were locked in their own struggles, unable to break free from the expectations that had been imposed on them. But Angela was determined not to let their unhappiness dictate her future. She knew what real happiness was now. It wasn't about wealth or status, but about having a few people who truly cared for you, like Jay and Maria.

Angela threw herself into her studies with renewed focus. She started visiting the local library in her spare time, researching everything she could about becoming a veterinarian. If she could get a head start, she knew she'd be more than prepared when the time came to apply for schools. She didn't want to be caught off guard like her parents, trapped in a life that didn't fulfill her. She was determined to carve out her own path, no matter how hard it was.

As summer approached, she felt a surge of excitement. It was more than just the thought of reuniting with Jay—it was the anticipation of returning to the world she was slowly making her own. A life that felt authentic, full of love and possibility. Angela knew, deep down, that one day this life would be hers permanently—not just for a summer escape but forever. Until then, she would prepare, she would dream, and she would make sure that nothing, and no one, held her back.

22

A year had passed, and it was finally time for Angela to return to the Hamptons. This time, however, the excitement was dampened by the strange turn her family had taken in the months prior. Her mother's mental health seemed to have deteriorated dramatically—Isabella had withdrawn from her social circles, locking herself away in their New York apartment. Whenever Angela tried to offer support, Isabella would snap, telling her to leave, insisting that she'd never understand. Angela's attempts to help had been rebuffed so many times, she had given up trying.

When she arrived at the Hamptons, her father and sisters were already there. To her surprise, her father looked different. Gone was the distant, distracted man she had grown accustomed to. Instead, he seemed lighter, almost carefree, with a spring in his step she hadn't seen in years. He even acknowledged her as she walked in, asking how she'd been. The warmth in his voice caught her off guard. It felt strange, like hearing from a stranger. Angela mumbled a brief response, still in disbelief, and hurried to her room to unpack.

As she sorted through her things, she caught sight of her parents outside by the pool. Their body language told her they were arguing, and curiosity tugged at her. She hesitated for a moment, then opened the window just enough to listen in.

"You have to help me!" Isabella's voice was frantic. "You have to call the police. This can't keep going on!"

Her father's voice, calm but cold, replied, "This is your mess, Isabella. I'm done cleaning up after you. You're not ruining my happiness again."

Angela's heart raced. What on earth were they talking about? Why did they need the police? And what did he mean by 'ruining his happiness'? None of it made any sense. She strained to hear more, but suddenly, the argument stopped. Her mother stormed off, slamming the door to the bedroom next to Angela's. She wondered if she should go to her, but after months of being shut out, she knew it was no use.

Her thoughts quickly shifted as Jay popped into her mind. She was just minutes away from seeing him again, and the excitement drowned out the tension from her parents' fight. She grabbed her bag and rushed to meet Maria, who was waiting to drive her to the beach cafe where she'd see Jay and their friends.

The next few hours were a whirlwind of party preparations—shopping for decorations, trying on clothes and swimsuits, and hunting for food and drinks for Jay's upcoming 18th birthday bash. It was a dream come true for Angela, to be back with her friends, laughing and enjoying the summer sun. Jay couldn't keep his hands off her, stealing kisses whenever he could, telling her how much he'd missed her.

"I can't wait for you to meet Joshua," Jay beamed, his face lighting up as he talked about his new baby brother. "He's the cutest little guy, and my mom and her boyfriend are so happy. You'll love them, Ella, and they're going to love you."

Angela smiled, feeling a warmth spread through her. Jay's happiness was contagious. But then he hesitated for a moment, his expression turning a bit more serious.

"I haven't told my mom too much about your life," he admitted. "You know how she feels about Hamptons folk. She can be a little... judgmental. I didn't want her to have any preconceived ideas about you. I'd rather she get to know you first. Is that okay?"

Angela nodded, understanding completely. Jay's Mother had always been wary of the wealthy summer crowd, and Angela wanted nothing more than to make a good impression. She appreciated that Jay hadn't shared too much about her background, hoping to build a connection with his mother without any barriers.

By the end of the afternoon, everyone was exhausted. Angela and Jay decided to slip away from the group for a quiet night together. They spent hours catching up, lying side by side, talking about everything and nothing, just enjoying the closeness they had missed during the long year apart. It amazed her how they could be separated for so long and still fall right back into their rhythm as if no time had passed.

They talked about the future—how Jay had been accepted into a school in New York and how they were already starting to plan their lives together. Angela felt a thrill at the idea of one day being together permanently, no longer just for the summers. They had even started talking about apartments and neighborhoods they wanted to live in. Everything felt so close, so possible.

As the evening drew to a close, Angela knew she had to head back home to rest before the big party and her long-awaited introduction to Jay's family. She wanted to look her best, make the right impression. But just as she was about to leave, Jay pulled her in close, his arms wrapping tightly around her. He stared into her eyes, his gaze soft but intense, as if he was seeing into her very soul.

Then, in almost a whisper, he said, "I love you, Ella."

Her heart skipped a beat. She couldn't believe what she'd just heard. Someone loved her—*truly* loved her. She felt like she might melt with joy. Wrapping her arms around his strong, wide neck, she leaned into him and whispered into his ear, "I love you too."

In that moment, nothing else mattered.

23

The day of Jay's 18th birthday party had finally arrived, and Angela could hardly contain her excitement. Maria woke her with a steaming cup of tea and a soft embrace, her eyes twinkling with shared anticipation. Over the past week, all the staff had been just as eager as Angela, helping her pick out the perfect outfit for the celebration. She wanted to strike the right balance—casual yet effortlessly stunning. Today, everything had to be perfect.

In her bedroom, one of the young maids gently applied Angela's makeup, accentuating her features with soft hues that made her deep blue eyes pop and her lips shimmer with a bold crimson red. Her dark hair fell in soft, natural curls, catching the morning light like a halo. When Maria stepped back to admire the final look, her expression softened in admiration. "You look so grown up, Angela. So beautiful... you remind me of your mother, the way she was when she was young."

The thought was a bittersweet one, but today, Angela felt radiant. All the staff gathered to hug her goodbye, Maria pressing a disposable camera into her hand as they sent her off with cheers. "Take lots of photos!" they shouted, waving from the driveway.

This was her moment. The one she had dreamed of for so long—the chance to meet Jay's family and, perhaps, feel what it was like to be part of a real family herself.

Angela's heart raced as she pulled up to Jay's new home. It was like something out of a fairy tale—a white picket fence surrounding the picture-perfect chocolate-box house. As she made her way through the garden gate, she found the party already in full swing. Laughter echoed from the pool where friends splashed about, and upbeat music played as people danced under twinkling lights strung through the trees. The air smelled of summer and fresh-cut grass, mingled with the sweetness of food sizzling on the barbecue. Casper bounded toward her, and she gave him a quick, affectionate squeeze before scanning the crowd for Jay.

By the garden table, Angela spotted a petite, elegant woman feeding a baby in a high chair. The woman's long, blonde hair glistened in the sun, and her kind, dark eyes— so much like Jay's—sparkled as she turned and saw Angela approaching. Without hesitation, she opened her arms wide and enveloped her in the warmest hug.

"You must be Ella," Jay's mother said, smiling so brightly that it made Angela feel at home instantly. "Wow, aren't you lovely?"

Jay stood a few steps back, watching them with a broad smile, his heart swelling with pride. His mother adored Angela, just as he knew she would. Angela greeted Jay's baby brother Joshua with a soft hello, admiring the little boy's chubby cheeks and wide, innocent eyes. Just as they were settling into conversation, Sophie appeared, her arms laden with decorations she had made herself.

"Come on, El!" she called, laughing as she handed Angela a drink. "Let me show you what I've done with the place."

Jay's mother watched them walk away and hugged her son close. "She's a keeper, darling," she whispered with a smile, and Jay beamed with joy.

As the sun dipped lower in the sky, casting the garden in a warm golden glow, Jay swept Angela into his arms, lifting her into the air as laughter bubbled between them. "She loves you!" he exclaimed, his voice full of happiness. "I'm so happy."

Angela, her heart full, asked, "Where's your mom's boyfriend? I still need to meet the whole family!"

Jay chuckled. "He'll be back soon—the bakery sent the wrong cake. They gave us one for an 8th birthday instead of 18!" They both laughed, unable to stop smiling.

The evening unfolded like a dream, the party pulsing with energy and joy. Angela stayed close to Jay, savoring every second of the night. It felt as though time had slowed just for them. They were inseparable, and she gazed up at him with adoration in her eyes, feeling a deep, unshakable connection between them.

For once in her life, something was utterly perfect. As they stood together, watching the crowd of friends and family laughing and dancing under the stars, Angela wished she could hold onto this moment forever. A deep sense of peace settled in her chest—this was where she belonged. Soon, they'd be in New York together, building their own future.

And for the first time, she realized with certainty that everything was exactly as it should be.

As Angela drifted off into her imagination, picturing the future she and Jay would build together, a chorus of "Happy Birthday" brought her gently back to reality. The crowd gathered as a massive birthday cake—nearly the size of a small child—was being carried towards Jay. The soft glow of dozens of candles illuminated the garden, casting flickering shadows across the party. Angela turned to watch, but something made her do a double take. The dim lighting made it hard to see, the brightness of the candles distorting her vision, but she was certain.

Her entire body froze.

Gripping tightly onto Jay's arm, Angela suddenly felt her legs wobble beneath her. Dizzy, she instinctively hid behind him, her heart pounding in her chest as if trying to escape. *This can't be real,* she thought desperately. She wanted to run, to flee the scene, but there was nowhere to go—she was surrounded by people. The crowd was closing in as the cake inched closer, everyone laughing and chatting without a clue that Angela's world was unraveling.

Sophie caught sight of her, noticing the panic in Angela's eyes, but the mass of people celebrating made it impossible for her to reach her. The guests cheered as Jay blew out the candles, basking in the joy of the occasion. Then, he turned towards Angela, beaming—until he saw her.

She was trembling, pale, her hands still gripping his arm like she was holding on for dear life.

"What's wrong?" Jay asked, his voice laced with concern, his eyes searching hers for an answer. Before he could react, there was a sudden crash.

The cake—once an elegant centerpiece—had slipped from the mom's boyfriend's hands, crashing onto the ground. A collective gasp rippled through the crowd as frosting and candles splattered across the guests. Jay's baby brother began wailing in the background, but all Angela could do was stare, frozen in place.

The world seemed to stop for a moment, the party fading into a blur. Then, in a voice barely above a whisper, Angela finally spoke, her words trembling as they escaped her lips as she looked at the man in front of her.

"Hello, Father."

Jay turned to her, confusion clouding his face. He hadn't processed what she had just said. His mother's expression turned to one of shock, her hands immediately going to soothe the now-crying baby. Daniel, her boyfriend, placed his face in his hands, as if the weight of the moment had just hit him like a ton of bricks.

But Jay... Jay stood there frozen, his mind reeling. He couldn't understand. He couldn't connect the dots.

Suddenly, Angela couldn't take it anymore. She bolted from the garden, her heart in pieces. Sophie, seeing the chaos unfolding, rushed after her, catching up to Angela just as she reached her car. Sophie slid into the driver's seat and threw the car into gear, speeding away as Angela dissolved into uncontrollable sobs beside her.

Huge, wracking sobs that shook her small frame. It felt like everything inside her was breaking apart all at once—years of pain, of heartache, all unleashed in a single, devastating moment.

Sophie drove in silence, one hand on the wheel and the other gently stroking Angela's hair, trying to offer some small comfort. But she knew that no words could fix what had just happened. All she could do was let Angela scream, cry, and vent her agony.

"Why?" Angela screamed, her voice cracking. "Why?! The one perfect thing in my life is ruined... gone. How could my father do this? How could he be here, *now*?" She gasped between sobs, her chest heaving as she struggled to catch her breath.

By the time they reached Sophie's house, Angela was exhausted—physically and emotionally. Sophie's parents were waiting at the door, worry etched across their faces. Without a word, Sophie's mother wrapped Angela in a tight embrace as soon as she stepped out of the car, holding her as if to shield her from the world.

Angela's body shook with grief as she buried her face into Sophie's mother's shoulder, feeling the overwhelming weight of her sorrow. A lifetime of pain seemed to pour out of her all at once. Her father's betrayal, the shocking revelation, the feeling of having lost everything that mattered—all of it flooded her heart until it felt like she couldn't breathe.

She had lost him. She had lost Jay and her father in one devastating blow.

And as she stood there, cradled in Sophie's mother's arms, the harsh reality sank in. The one perfect thing in her life—the one thing that had given her hope—was gone. In a world where she had been lost, Jay had been her compass. But now she would never find her way out of the darkness. All her dreams, her happiness, shattered in an instant. And in the hollow ache that filled her chest, Angela knew she could never undo what had just happened. She could only face the wreckage it left behind.

24

Days blurred together for Angela, who stayed at Sophie's house, cocooned in a protective silence. Sophie's parents had reassured her she could stay as long as she needed, and the phone never seemed to stop ringing—her mother, her father, Jay, their friends. But Angela didn't want to speak to anyone. She was numb. She sat by the window, staring out blankly at the world beyond, struggling to process everything that had happened.

How could she have never known her father had another life? Sure, he was rarely home, but she had always assumed he was busy running an empire. Now, it all felt like a cruel joke. And the future she had imagined with Jay, the one bright spot she had clung to, felt spoiled—just like everything else in her life.

She replayed every conversation she'd had with Jay about how incredible his mom's boyfriend was—kind, attentive, and so present in his life. It ate at her insides. How could this be the same man—her father? A man who had never shown her even a fraction of that love or attention, yet had been so devoted to Jay. The thought made her feel sick to her stomach.

The phone rang again. This time it was her sisters. Sophie knocked softly on the door, asking if Angela wanted to talk, but she only shook her head. Not now. Not yet.

Jay came by every day, knocking at the door, asking Sophie if Angela was ready to see him. But each time, she asked Sophie to send him away. It wasn't his fault—none of this was—but she just didn't have the strength to face anyone yet.

"Give her time," Sophie would tell him gently. "She'll come around."

On the fourth day, Jay left a letter for Angela. Sophie placed it on the dresser, where it sat untouched for hours. Angela couldn't bring herself to read it. She was afraid of what it might say. What if Jay wanted to break up with her? What if there were truths she wasn't ready to hear?

But as the day wore on, curiosity got the better of her, and eventually, she picked it up. Her heart raced as she unfolded the letter, her fingers trembling.

Dear Ella—or should I say Angela,

I know you don't want to see me right now, and I understand. I'll give you the space you need. But please, understand this—I'm just as shocked as you are. Please don't shut me out for too long. I want to help you, protect you from all of this. Nothing has changed for me, Ella. I still love you, and I still want us to live together in New York. We can make our own life, our own family.

After the party, I was furious. I demanded the truth from Daniel and my mum. I'm writing this to you so that there are no secrets between us—you can trust me. I know that must be hard under the circumstances, but here's what they told me, in their words, not mine:

Your father has been unhappy for longer than he can remember. He said he never really loved your mother, Isabella. Before he met her, he had just lost the love of his life—Annabel—a woman who left him when she found out she couldn't have children. He married Isabella because she was persistent, and when she became pregnant, there was no turning back. He was trapped in a life he never wanted, working all the time and distancing himself from your mother, who he said became difficult and self-centered.

He wanted to leave her, Angela. He tried many times. But she always threatened to ruin him, to take everything away. When the scandal happened—when he thought you were a boy—he felt humiliated and withdrew even further. He used his work as an excuse to escape.

Then, a few years ago, while selling your old Hamptons house, he met my mom. She was working as a secretary for the company that handled the sale, and they fell in love. He was honest with her about everything—about your mother, about you and your sisters. He told her how deeply unhappy he was, and they began their affair. He promised her he would leave Isabella. That's why my mom told me not to hang out with the rich folk- she wanted to prevent me ever meeting you or your sisters. But fate had different plans! When my mom found out she was pregnant, Daniel told your mother the truth. She had a breakdown, swore him to secrecy, and continued to threaten him if he ever left. At that point, your father hardly cared anymore. He now had a woman he loved, and nothing else mattered.

I know this is a lot to hear, and it must be painful. But I needed to tell you everything. Your father is ashamed of how he treated you. I confronted him about it, and he said he wants to make things right. It will take time, but we can get through this—together. You're stuck with me for life, Angela. We're family now. You can't get rid of me that easily. We share a brother, Joshua. He's your sibling just as much as he is mine. I love you, Angela, and I'll fight for you. Always.

You will forever be my Ella Bella.

Love always,
Jay x

Through her tears, Angela smiled, hearing Jay's voice in her mind, singing their song. She could picture him so clearly—her mind flashed back to them dancing under a huge umbrella in the summer rain, surrounded by their friends, laughing and spinning in the storm.

She read the letter again and again, trying to make sense of everything. Her life felt like a lie. The people she thought she knew—her parents, her family—were strangers. She felt lost, like she didn't even recognize herself anymore. But amidst the confusion and heartache, one thing was clear: she loved Jay, and she knew he loved her too.

With a pang of guilt, she realized how much she had shut him out. But she knew he understood. He always did. They were family now, no matter what.

Angela wiped her eyes, got up, and went to shower. She got dressed and made her way to the café, where Sophie's family was closing up for the day.

"Are you okay, darling?" Sophie's mother asked gently. "It's good to see you out."

Angela gave a small smile. "Do you mind if I make a milkshake and hang out for a bit? I needed to get out of Sophie's room—the walls were closing in."

"Of course, sweetheart," Sophie's mother replied, squeezing her shoulder. "We'll be just across the street if you need anything."

Angela nodded, feeling a bit lighter as she walked into the café. For the first time in days, she felt like she could breathe again. Though her world had shattered, there was a glimmer of hope—a promise that, maybe, she could piece it all back together.

It was dark now, and Angela sat in the empty café, the faint hum of the refrigeration the only sound breaking the eerie silence. She stared at her milkshake, its once cheerful swirl of colors now melted and lifeless. A strange feeling crawled up her spine—like someone was watching her. She shuddered, glancing nervously around. The café, which had once felt like a sanctuary, suddenly seemed too quiet. Too still.

Angela stood, walking toward the window, peering out into the inky darkness. The street was deserted, barely illuminated by a flickering streetlamp. Then, a noise. A faint shuffle, like someone moving just out of sight. Her breath hitched, her pulse quickening. She pressed her hand against the cold glass, trying to make out any movement in the shadows, but saw nothing.

She took a deep breath, shaking off the paranoia, and wandered toward the kitchen. It was probably nothing. Just her mind playing tricks on her after not sleeping much in days. She double-checked everything—the stove, the lights—and as she stepped back into the café, she froze.

Her parents stood by the door.

25

"Hello, Angela," they said, their voices unnervingly formal. They never called her anything affectionate—no "darling," no "sweetheart." Just Angela, like a business transaction.

Her heart stopped. She hadn't wanted to see them. Not now, not ever. She stared at them, her anger building beneath the surface, simmering hot.

"I don't want to see you," she said through clenched teeth, her voice trembling but edged with fury.

Her father stepped forward, his eyes pleading. "Please, Angela. We need to explain. We want to explain everything—to tell you the truth."

Angela glared at him, her voice cold and bitter. "You don't know the meaning of truth. You wouldn't know it if it hit you in the face! All this family knows is secrets and lies."

Just as he moved closer, the door behind him slammed open with such force that it rattled the entire café, and a deafening explosion echoed through the space—a sound so loud it shook the walls, like a bomb had gone off. Angela screamed as instinct took over, and she threw herself to the floor, her parents doing the same. Her father's arms wrapped around her protectively, something she couldn't remember him ever doing before.

For a moment, there was silence, except for the pounding in her ears. Her father's body shielded hers, and she could feel his heart racing as he clutched her close. She looked up, shocked at the unexpected tenderness, but before she could process it, she saw him.

Standing in the doorway was a tall man, holding a shotgun in one hand like he'd stepped straight out of a nightmare. He looked like something out of an old mobster movie—dark, slicked-back hair with streaks of grey, his face worn and weathered like he'd seen a lifetime of hardship. His eyes were cold, calculating. He was older than her parents, but there was something feral about him.

Her mother let out a strangled scream. "Marco—what are you doing?"

Angela's head spun. *Marco?* Who was Marco? Her mind raced—was he some distant relative, a family friend from Sicily? But before she could think any further, Marco stalked forward, grabbing Isabella by the arm and throwing her roughly to the floor.

Daniel, her father, began to rise in protest, but Marco simply raised the shotgun and pointed it at him, a silent threat that froze him in place. Her father raised his hands in surrender and backed down, pulling Angela closer, his voice low and trembling.

"Are we going to die?" Angela whispered, shaking uncontrollably. Her breath was shallow, her heart pounding so fast she thought it might burst.

Her father's arms tightened around her. He kissed the top of her head—another shock. "I'll protect you," he whispered, though his voice wavered.

Suddenly, Isabella's desperate cries filled the room as Marco screamed at her in Italian, his voice a thunderous roar. "Dov'è mio figlio?" Over and over, he demanded.

Isabella was sobbing hysterically, her voice frantic as she shouted back, "Non lo so! I don't know!"

Daniel glanced at Angela, his face pale, eyes wide with confusion. "What is he saying? What's going on?"

Angela struggled to remember the Italian lessons from her childhood, but her mind was fogged with panic. "I think... I think he's asking about a son."

Marco's fury grew with every second. He yanked Isabella up by her hair, the shotgun now pressed dangerously close to her face. Angela screamed, her voice piercing through the tense silence.

"Please! Please, stop! Don't hurt my mother- she doesn't have a son!" she begged, tears streaming down her face.

Marco's cold eyes shifted to Angela, his lip curling in a sinister sneer. "Do you even know what your mother has done?" he asked, his voice dripping with malice. "You rich little princess, sheltered from all the filth of your parents' lies. She hasn't told you about me, has she?" He turned his venomous gaze back to Isabella. "Snob. You let me rot in that cell. I thought you loved me, with all your money you could have come to free me."

Isabella shrieked, her hands flying to her head, trembling. "I only knew you for a few months, Marco! You never told me you were part of the mob—you lied to me!"

Marco's face darkened, the rage boiling over. "But you knew me well enough to have my son, didn't you?"

Isabella froze, her hands dropping to her sides, her entire body shaking. Daniel stared at her, his face twisted with confusion and pain.

"What... what is he saying, Isabella?" Daniel's voice broke as a tear slipped down his cheek.

Angela couldn't breathe. Her vision blurred as Marco's words sank in. *A son? Her mother had a son with... this man?*

Daniel's hand tightened around Angela's as the horrifying truth unraveled before them, but before anyone could speak, Marco's voice sliced through the silence.

"You abandoned me. You let me rot. But not anymore, Isabella. Not anymore."

Isabella looked ashamed as she saw the shock in her husband's and daughter's faces. Marco continued, his voice laced with bitterness, "I got out of jail eight months ago and have been looking for you—and my child—ever since. No one in our old neighborhood had seen you. They said you went back home years ago. Then, after months of searching, I ran into my cousin Tony. He said he used to see pictures of you in a magazine." Marco's eyes darkened with anger as he glared at Isabella. "And that's how I found you—one of the most powerful women in New York."

Isabella's voice trembled as she responded, the guilt weighing her down. "I knew you would come for me when I saw the headlines about your release. When I got your threatening letter, I begged you to help me, Daniel—but I couldn't tell you who he was. I know you just thought I was just scared of some mobster being released from prison." She looked down, her hands shaking, before continuing through tears, "I knew Marco would eventually come for me."

Angela's mind reeled as everything fell into place—her mother's strange behavior, the fear in her eyes, the sudden reclusion. It had all been building up to this moment, this horrible confrontation.

Isabella's voice cracked as she looked at Angela and Daniel, desperate to justify herself. "I don't owe you anything, Marco." She screamed, spitting in his face. She turned to Daniel "It was so long ago. I came to New York with nothing, a dream in my heart. But I didn't speak English, and no modeling agency would see me. Marco was there—he bought me gifts, treated me like I was his whole world. I was only sixteen, naive, swept off my feet. Then I found out I was pregnant." She paused, her words growing quieter. "A week later, I read the newspaper and saw the headlines: the man I thought I loved was a mobster, sentenced to life in prison. I went to Zia Rosa, and she took me to a convent to have the baby. I gave him away." Her voice broke as she whispered the last line.

Marco's face twisted with fury. "You did what?" he shouted, his voice growing louder with rage. "Where is he?" he screamed, stepping closer to Isabella, the tension in the room suffocating.

"I don't know!" Isabella cried, panic overtaking her. "The nuns arranged the adoption. I never saw him again."

Daniel stared at her, disbelief turning to anger. "Why didn't you tell me? You lied to me our entire marriage. All those years I wanted a son, and you failed to mention you'd already had one?" His voice rose with emotion, a tear running down his cheek.

Isabella lowered her gaze, barely able to meet his eyes. "I didn't tell anyone. I became Isabella Verona—the past was dead to me. I knew you'd never marry me if you knew. You'd see me as damaged goods."

Daniel's face hardened, his anger simmering. "But you knew I never wanted to marry you in the first place, Isabella. You trapped me in your lies, forced me into this life of deceit. I wanted a simple, honest life, and you poisoned everything."

Isabella's pleas were frantic now. "Please, Daniel. We were happy, sometimes, weren't we?"

He shook his head slowly, and Isabella crumbled before him, her voice trembling with regret. "I know I lost myself. I know I've done things I'm ashamed of. But everything was falling apart—my dreams, my life. I just tried to take control of something, anything."

Suddenly, Marco's hand whipped across Isabella's face with a sharp crack, sending her stumbling backward. Angela screamed, "Mother!" and tried to rush forward, but her father held her back, shielding her.

"You will pay for this, Isabella," Marco growled, seething with fury. His voice switched to rapid Italian, shouting accusations and demands that made Angela's stomach churn.

Angela stood frozen, her body trembling in shock. It was too much—the revelation about her father, her mother's dark past, and now this violent confrontation. Her entire life felt like a nightmare, a web of lies and betrayal. She was born into chaos, into a world built on secrets.

Amid the terror, Jay's face flashed in her mind—his loving smile, his comforting embrace. She longed for him, wished he were here to hold her, to tell her it would be okay. She felt safest when she was with him, like nothing could harm her. The panic deepened as she wondered if she would ever see him again.

But deep down, one thing remained clear. If she had the chance to see him again, she wouldn't let him go. He was her anchor, her truth in a life full of deception. Unlike her parents, Jay was the one good thing she could hold onto, the one person who gave her hope. He was her light in the darkness, and she would fight to keep him—no matter what.

26

Jay had been wandering the beach for hours, his thoughts consumed by Ella. The waves lapped against the shore, but his mind was elsewhere, replaying the past week and the letter he had written her. He hoped she had read it by now, processed everything, and would let him back in. He missed her more than he could express. The revelation of who she really was—Dan's daughter—had been a shock, but that wasn't what haunted him most. It was the fact that Dan, the man who had been like a father to him for years, was the same person who had hurt her so deeply.

Jay still felt utterly shell-shocked by the revelation. It didn't make sense—Dan had always been warm, kind, and generous toward him. He couldn't reconcile the man who had mentored him with the cold, distant father Ella had described. But as Dan had poured out his story, Jay began to understand. Dan had been lost and broken, carrying the weight of a life filled with pain. The loss of thinking he would have a son, the betrayal of his first love, and years of unhappy marriage had left him a hollow shell. Though it didn't excuse how he had treated Angela, it explained some of his actions. He had projected his pain onto her, seeing her as a reminder of all that had gone wrong.

But Jay knew better. He had seen Ella's kindness, her thoughtfulness, and her deep capacity for love. She wasn't like the shallow, surface-level woman her father assumed her to be- like Isabella and her sisters. Jay was determined to help them rebuild their relationship. They weren't so different, after all. They both loved animals, shared a sense of adventure and just wanted love in their lives. If only Dan would take the time to see it.

Unable to wait any longer, Jay's resolve hardened. He had to see her. He headed toward Sophie's house, where he hoped Ella might still be staying. Just as he was about to knock on the door, a deafening bang echoed through the air. Jay froze, his blood running cold. The sound was unmistakable—a gunshot. And it came from the direction of the café.

Panic surged through him as he sprinted toward the café, his heart pounding in his chest. Staying low, he crept up to the window, careful not to make a sound. What he saw through the glass sent a jolt of horror through him. A tall, dangerous-looking man stood inside, pushing Isabella to the floor while pointing a gun at Dan, who was huddled protectively around Ella.

Jay felt like he might pass out from shock, but adrenaline kicked in, sharpening his focus. There was no point in barging in—he'd only get himself killed. He needed help, fast. Without wasting a second, he bolted back to Sophie's house and pounded on the door, breathlessly explaining what he had seen.

Sophie's eyes widened as she grabbed the phone and dialed 911. "There's a man with a gun at my café. Hostages are inside—please hurry!" she said, her voice shaking.

Jay's pulse raced as he paced in the entryway, his mind reeling. Who was that man? What did he want? Maybe he was after their money. But Jay had no time to piece it together. Within minutes, police sirens echoed in the distance. They arrived at Sophie's house and quickly set up a perimeter, waiting for the SWAT team.

Jay explained everything to the officers—the gunman, the hostages, the terrifying scene he'd witnessed. The officers listened carefully, scanning the café with binoculars from a distance. They couldn't risk being seen. The man was armed, and they had no idea what he was capable of.

Ten minutes later, the SWAT team arrived. Jay watched as they started planning their operation, devising a strategy to take the gunman down and rescue the Hastings family. But then, a memory hit him—one that could change everything.

"The old garbage chute!" Jay exclaimed, startling the officers. "There's a secret passage into the café. We used to use it as kids to sneak in and out. It leads to the back of the building. You could get in that way, surprise him. He won't be expecting it."

The SWAT team leader's eyes narrowed as he considered the information. "Where's the entrance?" he asked.

Jay pointed toward a narrow alley behind the café. "It's hidden back there. I can show you."

The leader nodded, his mind racing with possibilities. "Alright. We'll send a team in through the chute. If this works, we might be able to end this before anyone gets hurt."

Jay's heart pounded as the officers moved into action, slipping into the shadows toward the secret passage. He had no idea how this would end, but one thing was clear: he wasn't going to stand by and do nothing. He would do whatever it took to save Ella.

27

Marco's grip on Isabella tightened as he yanked her toward the door by her hair. His face twisted with rage, eyes dark and wild. "I'm taking you and your daughter," he snarled, his voice a venomous hiss. "Daniel. You have 48 hours to get me $10 million and find my son, or I'll kill both of them. You're rich—use your fancy detectives, your contacts, whatever you've got. I want what's mine!"

Daniel's face crumpled in despair, tears streaming down his cheeks. "Please, no," he begged, his voice broken and desperate. "We can work this out. Just don't take them. Don't hurt them!"

Marco sneered, his lips curling in cruel amusement. "It's too late," he spat, his voice filled with cold finality.

The words cut through the air like ice. Angela clung to her father, her heart pounding in terror. Her legs felt like jelly beneath her, but she refused to let go of him. She'd never seen her father like this—so raw, so vulnerable. It made everything feel even more terrifying, like the world was collapsing around her.

Marco's hand shot out, grabbing Angela by the hair. She screamed in pain as he yanked her away from her father's arms. Daniel lunged forward, trying to hold on, but it was no use. Marco's grip was ironclad. He dragged both Isabella and Angela toward the door, their sobs echoing in the small café.

"If you come after me, I'll kill you too!" Marco shouted over his shoulder, his eyes filled with manic fury.

Then, with a chilling smirk, Marco raised his gun and fired a shot into the air. The deafening explosion seemed to tear through the room, reverberating through Angela's skull. Her ears rang, the world around her reduced to a high-pitched whine. The sound was disorienting, the sheer violence of it overwhelming.

Everything slowed to a crawl.

It was as if the world had stopped turning, and time was grinding to a halt. Angela blinked, her mind struggling to process what was happening when suddenly, shadows moved in the corner of her vision. Four figures, dressed in black from head to toe, stormed into the café through the kitchen. They moved with terrifying precision, like predators closing in on their prey. Angela barely registered their presence before they all raised their weapons in unison.

Four simultaneous shots rang out, the sharp crack of gunfire cutting through the tense silence. Marco's body jerked violently as the bullets ripped through him—one piercing his skull, another tearing into his chest, and the other two hitting his legs. His eyes went wide, blood splattering across the floor.

Angela's breath caught in her throat as she saw his already lifeless body begin to fall toward her, his large frame collapsing like a toppled statue. Panic surged through her, her limbs frozen in shock. Her mother leapt forward, throwing herself on top of Angela, shielding her as Marco's dead weight came crashing down.

The next few moments were a blur.

Police officers swarmed the café from every direction, shouting commands, their boots thudding against the ground. Isabella clung to Angela, sobbing uncontrollably as she wrapped her arms protectively around her daughter's trembling body and pressed a gentle kiss to her forehead. An officer grabbed Isabella, pulling her to safety, but Angela couldn't move—she couldn't breathe. The scene before her was too much, too surreal. Marco's lifeless form lay crumpled on the floor, blood pooling beneath him.

Daniel broke free from an officer's grasp and rushed toward Angela, his face pale with shock. "Angela!" he shouted, his voice thick with emotion as he pulled her into his arms. "I'm sorry, darling. I'm so, so sorry." His tears soaked into her hair as he held her tight, his body shaking with sobs. "I'll make this right, I promise. I'll never let anything happen to you again."

He held her as though she might slip away, his words a desperate mantra of regret and guilt. The world outside the embrace felt distant, like a bad dream. Angela clung to her father, her body still trembling, tears streaming down her cheeks.

Suddenly, she felt another pair of arms wrap around her and her father, pulling them both into a tight embrace. Through her blurred vision, she saw him—Jay. He was sobbing, his face pale, but his eyes full of relief. He pressed his lips to her cheek, his voice hoarse with emotion. "I thought I'd lost you. I thought you were gone."

Angela buried her face in his chest, her hands gripping his shirt. The fear, the tension, all the horror of the last hour began to unravel as she felt his warmth, his presence. She pulled back just enough to look into his tear-filled brown eyes, the love and fear swirling in them overwhelming her.

Jay kissed her softly, his lips lingering on her forehead. "I'm never letting you go," he whispered back, holding her tightly as if to anchor them both in the storm that had almost torn them apart.

For the first time in what felt like forever, Angela felt a flicker of hope, a light in the darkness. Whatever came next, she knew one thing for certain—Jay was her constant, her truth in a world full of lies. Just when she thought her life was crumbling around her and love was ending, she realised, this was where love begins.

"I'm not going anywhere," she whispered, her voice choked with tears. "I'm never losing you, Jay. Not ever."

Where Love Begins

Look out for the sequel, *Where Love Begins*, out now!

As Angela and Jay settle into their new life together in New York City, they're determined to build a future while helping to mend the broken ties with her family. But just as they start to find their footing, unexpected challenges and shocking revelations threaten to pull them apart.

Meanwhile, Isabella embarks on a personal mission to heal the wounds of her past and recover what she lost long ago—her son. Returning to her village in Sicily, she's faced with the heartbreaking consequences of leaving and vows to make amends for her mistakes.

Where one journey ends, another one begins. Join Angela and Isabella on an unforgettable journey of love, redemption, and the search for the one thing that matters most—family. *Where Love Begins* will have you hooked from the very first page.

Printed in Dunstable, United Kingdom

74719148R00097